I0822678

THE COTTON BROKER'S SON

HAP ROBERTS

a novel

First Printing, August 2025

Published by Roadhouse Books, LLC
Salisbury, North Carolina

Available in:
Hardback ISBN: 979-8-9851640-7-7
Paperback ISBN: 979-8-9851640-8-4
Digital ISBN: 979-8-9851640-9-1

Edited by Deirdre Parker Smith
Cover design by Andy Mooney
Back Cover Photo: Sean Meyers Photography ©
Book design by Sarah Michalec

Acknowledgements

John Brown
Elizabeth Cook
Elke
Steve Jacobs
Jeanette Lassiter
Lilli
Sean Meyers
Sarah Michalec
Andy Mooney
Wanda Peffer
Claudette Roberts
Deirdre Parker Smith
Susan Shinn Turner
Mark Wineka
Annette Roberts

Photo by Sean Meyers Photography

Finding a body

In the spring of 1957, Bobby Haskell cruised toward his favorite fishing hole in a cove on his buddy Bill Henderson's stretch of river. Bill had sunk a big old Christmas tree, weighted down with concrete blocks, into the muddy waters. It was an excellent spot to catch crappies.

The solitary fisherman had a cooler full of beer, a couple bologna sandwiches, several cans of Vienna sausages, and a sleeve of crackers. His wife Myra hated him to eat those "VI-eener" sausages, as she called them. Bad for his cholesterol. He didn't care. They'd been married 50 years, and he could do whatever he wanted — as long as she didn't know about it. He'd sneak a smoke and Moon Pie — bad for his blood sugar — in his garage workshop. Myra never went out there.

As Bobby cut his motor, he saw something floating in the water. It looked like some old clothes tangled in a familiar stump.

He got closer and ... Sweet Mother of God! Bobby leaned into the water and nearly threw up, his mind in disbelief and his stomach reacting immediately. He felt the world spinning.

It was part of a body floating in the water — and Bobby knew exactly whose it was by the size and what clothing was left.

This could be bad for the Henderson family.

Sam Miller Shoshonna

Tom Henderson Sr Susannah Henderson

(Tom Jr)

Preston Henderson Mollie Henderson

Morris Henderson Jenny Henderson

Hugh Davis Henderson Virginia Wright Henderson

William Thomas Henderson Elizabeth Benson Henderson

Bob Henderson Mindy Tanner Henderson

(Jennifer Henderson)

Photo by Sean Meyers Photography

Bob Henderson

Bob Henderson, the last of his family, steps back in time to tell stories about their past. He has closely studied his ancestry. Like so many of his forebearers, Bob's life is marked by tragedy, but his journey has been one of great discovery and success.

His great-great-great-grandfather, Tom Henderson, was not so lucky. He was killed in a lead mine explosion on May 1, 1839. He never even knew what hit him, the mine officials said. Only 29, he left a widow, Susannah, 28, and two sons, Tom Jr., 12, and Preston, 8.

For that family, everything changed in that instant.

Before the disaster, they'd sought a piece of the American dream. Settle on a plot of land, raise their boys, maybe some chickens and pigs and cows, plant a garden. Their shared dreams vaporized with a deafening roar.

In those days, lead mines were a profitable industry in the South. A valuable commodity, lead was used to make bullets. The lead business was a forerunner to the huffing, puffing, molten steel industry. But the mines were dangerous, and explosions were common, just as fatal accidents would become part of making steel.

Newspapers throughout the South covered the accident that killed Tom Henderson Sr. A reporter from the local newspaper wrote stories for five days straight, adding as many ghoulish details as he could. That's what the readers wanted and there was plenty to be found at the site.

Susannah took her husband Tom's death hard. She had no other family. Her father, Sam Miller, had been an avid outdoorsman who traveled West in the early 1800s to seek his fortune as a trapper. Sam fell in love with a Native American woman, Shoshonna. Although they were not allowed to marry, they lived together as man and wife.

When Shoshonna went into labor with their first child, Sam rode into town to fetch the doctor, but Doc Morgan refused to return with him because Shoshonna was Native.

Shoshonna died having that baby girl. But little Susannah survived. Tragedy followed the little family – times were tough, and people did what they could to survive. Sam died in a hunting accident a few years later. Folks who knew him said it was because of a broken heart. Susannah was sent to live with Sam's sister, a kind woman who'd never married. But Susannah was soon alone again when her aunt died. It was just before Susannah met Tom.

Susannah learned one thing through the losses – her mother, her father, her aunt, her husband. She had a strong will to survive.

Photo by Sean Meyers Photography

Susannah's story —1839

When Preacher Bob White and his wife, Evelyn, realized the struggle Susannah and her boys were facing, they stepped forward to help. The Whites lived in the large, rambling frame house next to the church.

Evelyn was an invalid, so the couple used only the downstairs. They'd converted the front room into a bedroom. It got lots of light and looked out over the expansive front yard and on to the mountains. Evelyn didn't leave the room much, but she was content. A quiet woman by nature, she loved to read her Bible on days she felt well enough. Other days she just rested and looked out the picture window. With the changing seasons, there was always something to see. Her husband was attentive to a fault.

The congregation loved Preacher White. He was gregarious and got a lot of mileage out of the fact that his name was the same as the bird's. Folks thought that was hilarious and he chortled right along with them — every single time, whistling the familiar bob white quail call. He was once considered handsome. But thanks to the many meals the church ladies had provided, his waistline had expanded to the point that he was portly.

For a big man, he was surprisingly light on his feet, stealthy when he wanted to be.

A few days after Tom's funeral, Preacher White went to visit Susannah and the boys.

"Evelyn and I have talked it over," he said. "We want you and your boys to stay in our home. We don't use the second floor, and we would appreciate your help with the housework and cooking in exchange."

This seemed like a godsend to Susannah, and she accepted immediately.

"Thank you so much, preacher. I knew the Lord would provide."

Although she easily passed for a White person, Susannah had her mother's dark hair and eyes. No one in town knew her family background. It wasn't obvious, because her hair was not black and straight, but chestnut brown and wavy, like her father's. Like her mother, she was beautiful. You couldn't help but notice — Preacher White certainly did Sunday after Sunday from the pulpit. Even though she did nothing to attract his attention, he was bewitched by her from the start, even before her husband was killed.

He didn't have wicked thoughts when asking Susannah and her boys to come and live with them. He did like the idea of having a pretty, young woman to look at now and then. The devil worked on him later.

The young family's move came about the time Louis Daguerre started experimenting with photography.

In 1838, he got credit for the first photograph of a person on the streets of Paris. Suddenly, photography became a worldwide sensation. Pornography, also a French invention, came shortly after.

Preacher White fancied himself a worldly and well-read man, despite the small parish he served in the North Carolina mountains.

He traced his lineage to France, and still had cousins there he corresponded with occasionally. In one letter, his cousin Pierre enclosed some postcards of scantily clad women as a joke. Today, they'd be considered quite staid, but in that time, they caused a stir.

Preacher White couldn't take his eyes off the women on the postcards, especially since one reminded him of Susannah. His poor Evelyn had been sickly for so long. He wrote back, asking Pierre to send more postcards "for the historical value" they'd have one day. Pierre saw right through the preacher's ruse but kept it to himself. He got a kick out of it.

Preacher White soon amassed quite a collection. The postcards were easily produced, inexpensive, and popular. He was a leg man, and the creamy white thighs he saw sent him into heights of ecstasy. He envisioned what Susannah would look like in the provocative poses. He put it out of his mind. Then the thoughts would recur. Soon, he could think of nothing else. The preacher was not a bad man, he thought to himself, but these thoughts were not good. He prayed for guidance but could not erase the images from his mind. Because Susannah worked in the garden and house, Evelyn told her, "There's no need to wear your Sunday best all the time." She knew Susannah didn't have many dresses, and she didn't want them to wear out too quickly.

"You can wear some of my old house dresses," Evelyn said. They had none of the under layers the ladies usually wore. That suited Susannah fine; those fancy dresses of the day were too much. "Miss Evelyn, thank you so much. It will make it easier for me to work if I don't have to worry about mussing my good dresses." She also loved being outdoors and tanned beautifully.

Such natural beauty, and the look of his Evelyn's dresses on the young lady finally drove the preacher over the edge.

That summer, he hatched a plan which would give him the secrecy he craved.

The church and parsonage shared a cellar that hadn't been cleaned since the couple had been there. Evelyn couldn't do anything about it. Parishioners often brought canned goods, and the cellar was the perfect place to store them.

Several hams were already hanging from the low rafters — one parishioner raised hogs and made sure the Whites always had a nice ham. Preacher White had learned to make decent biscuits, and the congregation clamored for his ham biscuits during covered-dish dinners.

"I hate to ask this," Preacher White said to Susannah, "but would you help me clean the cellar?"

Evelyn's house dresses were a little tight and a little short on Susannah — much to his secret delight — and it didn't matter if they got dirty. Like every other task she was asked to perform, Susannah accepted the request in her usual sweet manner.

The cellar was packed with shelves and boxes; adding the preacher's ample girth made it even tighter. It didn't take terribly long to clean up the place, but Preacher White chatted with Susannah, trying to gain her trust and make her feel comfortable. When the cleaning was finished, thanks to Preacher White stretching out the time — and the fact they only worked on Fridays, his day off — Susannah offered to organize the shelves.

"Now that we have cleaned up, I'd like to re-arrange the shelves so you can find things better."

"I don't want you down here alone," the preacher answered. "It's not safe."

The truth was, he didn't want her down there without him. Whatever his inappropriate thoughts were, he wanted no harm to come to her – that's what he told himself.

Susannah couldn't imagine what wasn't safe about the place, but she soon found out. Preacher White was the danger she needed protection from.

One Friday, he said, "I don't want you to think I'm evil or have evil in me, but I cannot get over your beauty, Sister Susannah."

She started to smile, but did not speak. Then he said, "Take off your dress."

Susannah froze. Maybe she didn't understand?

"If you and your sons want to continue to stay here, take off your dress."

She did as she was told, revealing a thin cotton camisole and plain bloomers beneath.

To anyone else not starved for affection the way the preacher was, her plain clothing may have seemed simple and not sexy in the least. With Susannah's perfect figure, the preacher was extremely excited.

At first, he simply watched her work. The next week, he asked the same of her. And the same as the weeks rolled past. She said nothing because he had threatened her family, though her resentment was growing. Finally, he needed more. He knew he could never have relations with her as she was still of childbearing age. How would such a pregnancy be explained? His congregation were simple folk, but even they wouldn't buy an immaculate conception.

After a few weeks of watching, he became emboldened. That Friday afternoon in the cellar, he walked behind her and started rubbing himself against her. Susannah drew in a sharp breath and went still as a statue. She closed her eyes, tight. She responded in no way whatsoever. At first, the preacher was enraptured. Then he realized he may as well have been rubbing up against a cold stone.

All the air left the room.
He fled the cellar and hustled to his small study at home, closing the door quietly so as not to disturb Evelyn's nap, and found relief in the dark, alone.

This practice, too, went on for several more weeks. Neither he nor Susannah said a word after that afternoon in the cellar. He felt enormous shame, but neither could he stop.

Susannah remained pleasant but distant, quiet. She barely spoke to anyone. What had been a cordial friendship was now ruined, thanks to him, and she was deeply afraid of what he could do to her and her boys.

He tried to cut back on the abuse. At his request, Susannah still helped him prepare communion on Friday afternoons. He kept his distance — most of the time.

Months and then years passed.

Susannah prayed every night, "Dear Jesus, help me protect my children and raise them right. If it be your will, take this evil man's desires away from me and show him the way of truth. Lord, forgive me for what I've done and help me find a way out."

Susannah — still as beautiful as ever — never knew when the preacher would put his hands on her. Never at the home, always over at church. Trying to reason it out, she thought, "Perhaps he thinks he is being absolved by being on holy ground." But she knew he was damning himself to Hell. Like the Virgin Mary, she kept her own counsel. She was devoted to her sons and had no close friends since she spent all her time working for the Whites.

Then the unthinkable happened.

Susannah had insisted her boys stay in school after their father died, and the Whites supported her decision. Before her illness, Evelyn had been a teacher and believed in the value of a good education. She dreamed the boys would even go to college one day. They were both bright. She and Preacher White had already discussed sending them. They were going to tell Tom as his graduation gift. He'd dropped "Junior" as soon as his father died. He was the man of the house, he told his grieving mother.

Outside of keeping their rooms neat, helping clean up after meals, chopping wood, and raking the yard and keeping it neat, Tom and Preston had few duties. The preacher didn't have any livestock; he spent all his extra time caring for his wife. Along with the hams, his parishioners provided the Whites eggs, chicken, and occasionally, beef.

One afternoon after chores, the boys were outside playing catch. At 17 and 13, they loved to be outside and play ball together. Despite the four-year age difference, they were close. Preston idolized his big brother, always had. Tom would be out of school soon, so they were relishing the time left before he started work at the cotton mill in town. Susannah insisted that he graduate from school and had the same plans for Preston.

Suddenly, Preston launched the ball over Tom's head. The kid was getting quite an arm on him, Tom thought to himself. He just needed a bit more control. The ball landed beside the cellar door in the churchyard.

"Be right back!" Tom hollered as he jogged over to fetch it. He was tall and lanky like his father yet carried himself gracefully like his mother.

While waiting, Preston laid down in the yard, his hands behind his head, and studied the puffy clouds in the blue sky. His mother had taught him to look for shapes. It was one of his favorite things to do.

Tom was in a good mood. Graduation was weeks away, and he'd be able to help his mother with a real income.

As Tom knelt to grab the ball, he heard what sounded like moans coming from the cellar. He knew from his mother about Native American tradition, and he respected it. He also knew there were no such things as ghosts. He cocked his head and listened more intently. He suddenly realized that was no ghost. That was a man's voice. Preacher White! Tom dropped to his belly, inched over to the window and peered in. What he saw made him sick. He wanted to burst in and break Preacher White's neck, then and there. But he also knew — as furious as he was — it would hurt his brother and most of all, their mother.

Instead, he hollered as loud as he could, "Hey, Preston! Here it is! You sure threw it a long way!"

He listened again. The noise had stopped.

Momentarily relieved, he jogged back over to Preston. He'd bide his time.

For now.

"C'mon, let's go get the fire ready for Mother to start supper."

"Can't we throw a little more?" Preston asked. He was a great kid, obedient to his mother and brother.

"Not today. But I have a surprise for you tomorrow," Tom said.

"All right!" Preston said, pumping his fists.

When Susannah came into the kitchen, Tom acted as if he'd seen or heard nothing. Preacher White was his usual jovial self. The big, fat fake. Tom seethed inwardly. He wanted to kill the preacher where he stood. Instead, he took some deep breaths and set the table.

The boys helped their mother finish preparing the meal. She was unusually quiet. Tom even took Evelyn's tray to her and ate with her, as he did sometimes. She was surprised but glad for the company. He couldn't face Preacher White — but soon.

Before bed that night, Tom went into his mother's room. She was brushing her long hair before braiding it. That was the sole bit of self-care she allowed herself. One hundred strokes per evening. He sat down on the other side of the bed and watched her. He wasn't sure exactly what to say.

He waited until Susannah finished tying her braid. He had to wait a while.

"What is it, Tom?"

"Mother, I know. And I'm betting what I heard today wasn't the first time."

Susannah opened her mouth as if to respond, then closed it. She sat quietly for a while, choosing her words carefully. When she finally spoke, tears glimmered in her eyes.

"You're right, Tom. It's been going on for a while. I hope that you understand I don't have a choice. He threatened to kick us out. We have nowhere else to go," her voice cracked. "I pray and pray for us to be free of this awful burden."

"I think we have a way. I'm taking you and Preston into town tomorrow. He and I are going to talk to Mr. Estes, the mill foreman. They're coming into busy season so they're hiring. I stopped by the hotel to talk with Mr. Johnson since his son George is my best friend. He and Mrs. Johnson are selling the hotel, and the new owner wants to hire a housekeeper and cook's assistant. I told Mr. Johnson you'd be the perfect person. He thinks a lot of me and said he'd be glad to introduce you to the new owner, Mr. Littlejohn, who will be in town tomorrow morning. Don't worry, Mother. We'll get out of here as soon as we can."

"Oh, thank you, Tom," Susannah said as the tears rolled down her face. "I knew we would be able to escape one day!"

"Escape?"

"Well, yes. To me, this has felt like a prison."

That made Tom feel even worse, but he didn't say anything. He gave his mother a big bear hug, then went to his room.

The next morning, Preacher White graciously let Tom take the horse and buggy into town. He thought they were going for coffee, sugar, flour, and other provisions.

He was partly right.

Susannah met with Jacob Littlejohn, who was immediately enchanted by her — as was Juanita, his wife and helpmeet. They offered her a job on the spot to include room and board for her and her boys. After all, they cooked and served three meals a day, so she was needed at the hotel.

Meanwhile, at the mill, Clayton Estes talked with both boys. Preston had told Tom he'd tag along, but he was secretly determined to be hired, too. Tom was surprised when Mr. Estes offered Preston a job as well, but he knew there was no way his little brother wasn't going to pull his weight. As far as Preston was concerned, his school days were over, no matter what Mother said. Tom had to agree with him. He hadn't told Preston why they were leaving.

By lunchtime, the three of them had jobs.

"Please don't say anything, Tom," Susannah said. "I need time to get our clothes clean and packed. I also want to give the house one final deep cleaning, for Evelyn's sake." It was time for spring cleaning, so she wouldn't arouse the preacher's suspicion.

Mr. Littlejohn said he would come for them the next Friday,

Good Friday. Thank goodness they wouldn't have to walk, although Susannah would have gladly crawled.

On Good Friday, Susannah went to the church to prepare communion. This morning, however, her step felt lighter, her strength renewed.

She first thanked God, "Lord Jesus, thank you, thank you. I dedicate my life to you always. Bless my boys and help us in this new life." She'd made it.

She went a little earlier than usual to leave bouquets of white daisies in the sanctuary for an Easter service she wouldn't attend. She'd never darken that doorway again as long as Preacher White was in town.

She'd told Tom what time she was headed over to church. As the preacher was shaving, Tom slipped over to the cellar and hid in the shadows, waiting.

The flowers arranged to Susannah's satisfaction, she steeled herself to go down to that dreaded cellar one last time. It would always be horrific to her. This time she knew she had an ally.

She took a deep breath, then opened the cellar door. Sure enough, the preacher was already down there. Susannah tried to act normally and reached for the bottle of muscadine wine a parishioner faithfully prepared. Then the preacher was behind her, his breath hot on her neck.

"I don't know that you want to do this, Preacher," she said quietly.

"Why not?" he sneered. "I've been doing it for years."

Suddenly, a deep voice came from shadows.

"She's right. Step away!"

"Who's there?" Preacher White asked, startled.

"Who do you think it is?"

Tom stepped into the light. Something glinted in his right hand. He'd recently had a growth spurt, and he towered over the preacher. The preacher was scared. He realized things had gone horribly wrong. Then he saw what was in Tom's hand — a switchblade.

"I really want to castrate you right now," Tom said, as the preacher began to tremble. He knew Tom was dead serious. "And then you'd beg me to slit your throat."

He paused for several moments to let the words sink in, for the preacher to consider his options.

"Instead, the three of us are leaving — today. We all have jobs and a safe place to live."

"But you're all safe here..."
Tom made a growling sound.

The preacher was trembling, and Tom smelled the acrid smell of urine. He laughed bitterly and took a step closer.

"That's what I thought for years. I was wrong. I was a child. Now I am a man. And I know right from wrong. So here's what's going to happen. We are leaving. We will not be back. Except for one thing. If I get the slightest hint you've done this to another woman, I will be back. And I'll bring this knife."

The preacher could only nod.

"C'mon, Mother," Tom said, reaching for her hand. He and Susannah exited the cellar for the last time, into the bright sunlight.

A new chapter — Spring 1844

It didn't take long for Susannah and her sons to get settled at the hotel. She liked her job. She was used to working — and a small hotel wasn't much harder to keep clean than a large house. The guests loved her, as did the Littlejohns. Having had no children of her own, the matronly Mrs. Littlejohn took the small family under her prodigious wings.

The work at the mill was hot and dirty, but the boys didn't complain. They worked hard and were promoted steadily. Preston, especially, kept his head down and stayed as close to his brother as possible.

The family flourished, at least for a few years. Then the strain of the mill work and what his mother had been through finally got to Tom, and he started drinking.

At first, he was able to keep it a secret. As his drinking escalated, he showed up to his shift drunk as a skunk. The first couple of times it happened, Mr. Estes gave him a second chance, and then a third.

Until there were no chances left.

Mr. Estes called him into his office one morning. "Tom, I'm sorry. I'm going to have to let you go. This equipment is dangerous enough as it is. I'm giving Preston your job. Get yourself together. Your mother raised you better than this. Stop drinking. If you can do that, I'll have a job for you."

"Yes, sir, thank you, sir." Tom was polite to the last.

But it was not to be.

Instead, Tom ran away and found work at a circus. Preston got postcards from him over the years from this town or that. Some places he'd heard of; some he hadn't. He kept every card. No matter what, he still loved his brother and looked up to him. Tom's favorite job was taking care of the elephants. They were behemoths, but they were gentle with you if you were gentle with them, Tom wrote. On particularly bad nights, Tom would stumble into the stall of his favorite beast, Doris, and sleep a dreamless sleep.

Sometimes, Tom would cry in his sleep; he felt what he thought was his mother's hand on his forehead. Instead, he'd wake to find it was Doris, gently caressing his forehead with her trunk, easing him back to sleep. None of the other workers believed it until they saw it for themselves. Whatever the reason for his tears, he cried many nights. Doris was always there.

It's true what they say: An elephant never forgets. Neither could Tom. His drinking dogged him — the proverbial monkey on his back. He worked with the circus until he was no longer physically able — an old man before his time. He bid farewell to Doris and the other elephants. Doris cried, tears streaming down her kind, gray face. He said so long to his fellow workers. He came home broken but determined to contribute somehow to his family.

Preston, who was now a foreman and lived with his own young family close to the hotel, let Tom have their spare room. Tom was no trouble, unless he got on a drinking binge.

When Tom was sober — which was becoming more common, Preston noticed — he'd do odd jobs around town, mucking out the stables, delivering groceries and whatnot.

Preston prayed that Tom could turn his life around. Then Tom would get paid, which started the cycle all over again. Finally, Preston had to take Tom's money and give him a small allowance and absolutely keep him out of the hotel's adjoining saloon. The Littlejohns didn't want him drinking and neither did the barkeeper, a classmate of Tom's from school. It was bad for business to have an employee's son passed out in the corner.

Susannah and Preston thought he was improving, until the effects of alcoholism started taking over his body. It was hard to watch.

Late one afternoon, Preston came in from the mill and found Tom in bed, still in his pajamas. This never happened, even when Tom was drunk.

"Come here, brother," Tom said as Preston sat on the bed and took his outstretched hand.

"I don't have much time." His skin was jaundiced, and Preston knew he was beyond help this side of heaven. "There's something you need to do for me."

"Anything."

His brother seemed to be slipping away already.

“Take care of Mother. Protect her.”

“Of course I will. From what?”

“I failed her before.”

“Before?”

“With the preacher.”

Preston kept holding his brother’s hand. This wasn’t making sense. Until it did.

“I talked to him before we left that day. I doubt he’ll bother her again. In fact, I’m sure of it.”

“Oh, I’ll make sure of it, brother.”

Preston squeezed his brother’s hand. Tom smiled faintly, nodded, and closed his eyes. Preston sat by his bedside all night.

When Preston woke up the next morning, Tom was gone. He was only 35.

Not long after, Evelyn White died. She must have pieced together what had happened between the preacher and Susannah, and it broke her heart. The morning after her funeral, Preacher White left town and was never heard from again. He didn’t say goodbye to his congregation, which eventually learned what had happened – or a version of it. Preston remained vigilant for months, until it was clear White wasn’t coming back. He and his mother breathed sighs of relief. True to her word, Susannah returned to church and was greeted with open arms. The congregants were not so simple after all.

Susannah and Preston were truly free.

As the years wore on and Susannah grieved for her two Toms, her mind often turned to what an arduous journey she had been on. Sometimes she wondered if all the death and tragedy in her life were some sort of punishment for the way she was born.

But most of the time, she felt thankful that she still had Preston and a place to work and live. She loved Preston's children so much and just wanted them to have better, easier lives. If she could see them happy and successful, she would feel her suffering had been worth something.

Photo by Sean Meyers Photography

The War of Northern Aggression

Bob had to do a lot of research to find out much about his great-great-great-grandmother after her husband died beyond the early newspaper clippings of the lead mine explosion. Then he hit the jackpot when it came to the letters Susannah's surviving son, Preston, and his son wrote to their loved ones during the Civil War.

Bob's great-great-grandfather and his great-grandfather both fought for the Confederacy. How, you ask? Easy. It happened because of a lie.

At around 30 years of age, Preston Henderson, Bob's great-great-grandfather, was practically considered an old man, but he volunteered to fight because he felt it was his duty — even though he was married with children. He and his sweet Mollie had four sons. Just after his brother Tom died, he signed up.

Preston's oldest son, Morris, was born July 4, 1850. He lied about his age to fight from 1864 to 1865. He was Bob's great-grandfather.

Preston never owned slaves but did believe in states' rights. The War started when Confederate troops fired on and took over Fort Sumter on April 12, 1861. North Carolina and South Carolina were part of 11 states that formed the Confederate States of America on Feb. 8, 1861.

Before war broke out, Preston left the mill and bought a small general store with an attached feed mill. He left it to Mollie and their boys to run as he walked off to join the War. Morris joined him in battle. Father and son eventually walked back home and resumed their lives. Preston became one of the first storekeepers to extend credit to the freed Black slaves. He also armed them so that they could protect themselves. The Klan came to Preston's house twice and threatened to kill him. He pulled out his sawed-off shotgun.

"Don't bother me and don't bother my customers," he growled. "That includes people sleeping in the woods. They got teeth. They'll fight you. They're not gonna take it like they did when they were slaves."

He was right.

There were confrontations between the Klan and freed slaves. Some Klan members were killed. Because of the kind of man Preston Henderson was, however, there was no retribution from the families. They knew he had a lot of backup in those woods, and in the community.

The store was successful, a community hub, but not a big money maker. Preston's son Morris encouraged his own son to become a cotton broker. That set the trajectory for Bob's family's life as he knew it.

One of Bob's idols, his grandfather Hugh Davis Henderson, Morris' son, was born Dec. 3, 1896. Morris was 45 then, and his wife, Jenny, was 40. Hugh was the baby.

Cotton mill life

Like most folks after the War, Hugh had to grow up fast. He went to work at Benson Cotton Mill when he was just 10. He fetched bolts of cloth from the prep area once they had been cleaned and woven and carried them over to the women in the finishing area. Within a month of starting work, he could carry his weight in a bolt. It would cause him back trouble later in life, but as a youngster, he got along okay.

The foreman liked Hugh and had a special cart for him to use that was just his size.

The women in the finishing area doted on Hugh. They'd bring leftovers from the large meals they cooked for their families, which, all combined, tasted delicious to a young boy. A smorgasbord. That was pretty much what he ate until he got home at night. Hugh didn't complain. He loved the attention and was always appreciative of whatever he got.

The women at the mill also gave him scraps of cloth. His dear mother worked magic with a needle and thread. Hugh had warm quilts to sleep under during the dark, cold winters, thanks to her and his friends at the mill.

He married Virginia Wright, a daughter of one of the ladies he worked with, the day they both turned 18.

William Thomas "Bill" Henderson was born three years later in 1917. But Virginia died in the flu pandemic of 1918. Hugh never talked about her, but everyone knew he must have loved her deeply. Hugh never remarried. A heart murmur kept him from serving in World War I.

Photo provided by the Davie County Public Library

Carpetbaggers during Reconstruction

Hugh was grateful for his job at the mill. On Sunday afternoons, he told Bob years later, the Henderson adults talked about the Benson family. Most of the talk was negative — even to a boy's ears.

Adolph Benson had heard stories of the South in poverty at the end of the War. His family lived in Ohio, and he escaped serving in the War. He was a Yankee through and through. He talked his aging grandfather into loaning him some money. He wanted to see the South in dire straits for himself, up close and personal. Twist the knife as much as possible.

Adolph left home at 18 and ended up in a small village in North Carolina. He heard of a family who owned a cotton mill and a large farm, but all the Daniels men had been killed in the War. Sherman's boys came through and burned their homeplace. The cotton mill was suffering, too, shut down and damaged by the Union general. To make matters worse, the carpetbaggers took over local government and raised property taxes, so all was lost of the Daniels family. Still, everyone in town remembered and greatly admired them.

This was the scenario young Adolph had dreamed of. He became an ally of the carpetbaggers. He did whatever needed to be done. Over the next several years, he ended up with the mill and the land — all that had once belonged to the Daniels family. He also married a carpetbagger's daughter whose family had taken control of the local bank. The bank received a grant from the federal government, and Adolph and his family, the Bensons, began their life in the "New South."

Photo by Sean Meyers Photography

The Retreat's genesis

Just after Hugh married his dear Virginia, he started buying land for a hunting lodge he named The Retreat. He didn't know what he wanted to do with the land — replant some trees in conjunction with the North Carolina Forest Service and maybe put in some crops at some point. He was only 18 and World War I had just started. But he knew they weren't making any more land.

In the 1920s, Alcoa started buying up land to build a reservoir and construct dams for its smelting operations. One of Hugh's high school buddies, Clifford Marsh, was the real estate manager for Alcoa. His job was to approach farmers to sell what land would become waterfront property. The farmers were paid far more than what the land was worth, $100 an acre on average. After all the purchases were completed, the company turned around and sold the surplus for $10 an acre. Cliff also handled those transactions. Hugh jumped on that immediately, eventually amassing 2,000 acres. The Henderson property backed up to Lake Snyder, the newly created reservoir.

When the war ended, the cotton market decreased dramatically. With the frantic pace of the commodity market shifting down, it gave Hugh the freedom to focus on his other investments.

Hugh would go to his office first thing, approve invoices, answer his mail, and dictate any correspondence to Betty.

He bought a surplus four-wheel-drive Jeep to drive around the farm's property lines to find out what other property was available for sale. He hired some veterans to dig the post holes for fencing with a separate line of barbed wire at the top.

Hugh thoroughly enjoyed seeing the property come to life. With the vets' help, he had a gravel drive put in stretching out to the main road, secured with a double gate he kept open during the day and locked with a stainless-steel, heavy-duty chain and sturdy padlock at night.

He put out a mailbox to get mail at Route 1, Box 10, Magnoliaville, NC. He was giddy as a schoolboy when the first letter came.

The original property came with a small farmhouse and a few cabins. He renovated everything first class, knowing he'd have to hire a property manager and housekeeper as he added acreage.

Bill, Hugh's son with his dear Virginia, had grown up in the farmhouse until his father built a spacious new, two-story log cabin they called The Lodge in the early 1940s.

Off to Woodberry

As soon as he was able, Hugh started putting money away toward his son's education. Hugh had an insatiable curiosity to learn. He wished he had gone further in school, but he was determined to learn from the school of life.

He told Bill, "Every Sunday after church, I walked down to the library to read the newspapers."

Hugh had the intelligence to go to college but had to quit school to work in the mill. He understood how it was. Hugh worked hard. He continued to advance at the mill until he was promoted to supervisor of raw materials.

He learned all facets of the mill's operation while learning about the world through newspapers. He learned from folks at the mill, too — common-sense advice, the kind of information you can't find in books. They'd talk. He'd listen. He never realized his dream to go to college, but he was damned sure Bill would go. This was how he raised Bill, so he never thought anything different would happen.

When Bill was about to enter the ninth grade, Hugh decided to send him to Woodberry Forest in Virginia, a boarding school. Bill was thrilled for the opportunity to better prepare himself for college through prep school. He and his father had already determined that he'd go to N.C. State College in Raleigh to study how to manage the family's land.

Bill met interesting and influential people during his time at Woodberry. He went to class and lived with the sons of tobacco company owners, major bankers, entrepreneurs, philanthropists, legislators. It was the place to be for those who already had a bright future ahead, and for those who needed the education and the relationships with the sons of industry and commerce.

While the Hendersons had money and did well in the business world, some of Bill's classmates were far richer and better placed for success. Bill figured out quickly who was important and who was useful. He also developed a core of solid friends, regardless of their status.

Bill found his group quickly – ambitious, smart, curious young men who honestly wanted to improve themselves.

Richard became a close friend. His father Edward Mitchell had been fascinated by airplanes, with the very idea of a machine being able to move through the air and devoured everything he could about the Wright brothers. He chose the name Richard for his boy. He visited Nags Head to see the origin of flight and even traveled to Ohio to meet the Wright brothers. Of course he took Richard, his only son. He had very high expectations — he remembered his own education and reading "Don Quixote," with the famous quote, "the sky's the limit."

That's all he wanted for Richard.

Richard, in turn, loved everything his father did. Flying was almost an obsession. Bill shared that obsession with him.

Two other boys at the school, Howard and Gerald, joined their flight-hungry friends. Gerald's family had a long history in engineering, so he learned a lot just by hanging out at the manufacturing plant that made engines of all kinds.

Richard came from the coastal plains, flatland. Gerald came from Raleigh, the state capitol. Howard was from the tobacco town of Winston-Salem.

Gerald and Howard came from big families that were counting on their sons to keep up a tradition of success. They supported anything that seemed new and on the cutting edge.

Richard had a sister whose prospects were good. He figured he'd wrestle the most he could out of life and make his old man proud.

When they were approaching summer break, Richard didn't want to leave his friends, so he asked Bill what his plans were.

"I guess I'll go home and help my father with his business," Bill said.

"Didn't you tell me you wanted to study agriculture?" Richard asked.

"I do. We have a 2,000-acre farm in McNeill County. I'm planning to study agriculture and forestry at State to learn how to plan for the future."

"I have an idea," Richard said. "You can spend the summer with me — we have 800 acres of farmland, and I'd rather work it with you than some of the guys my father brings in. They can be a rough bunch."

"I don't know," Bill said, thinking of his father and their land that needed working.

"Well, I know something you don't. You keep saying you want to learn to fly. Dad has a biplane, and he wants me to take flying lessons."

"Really? I've always wanted to fly! Dad loves flying. You think your family would really let me do that?"

"My dad pretty much agrees with whatever I want to do," Richard said. He wasn't smug about it, as far as Bill could tell. It seemed like he really wanted them to spend the summer together.

"Come on," Richard said, "let's write to our dads and get it all settled. I bet my mom will get a kick out of having another kid in the house, and it will irritate my sister!"

Bill smiled and crossed his fingers. He was already excited, and he knew his father wanted him to have new experiences and learn things that would be useful in the future. Both he and his father thought flight was going to be important and it would make his dad proud if he learned to fly.

Flying for the whole family

Hugh was interested in flying but never had the chance to get his pilot's license. He'd just turned 17 when the Wright Brothers went up for the first time on Dec. 17, 1903. He wanted to experience the thrill himself someday.

Flying captured his whole being. He knew that someday, somehow, he would fly. He was too poor to take flying lessons, but there was Bill, full of possibilities.

Bill got an answer to his letter right away. His father had a lot of questions, but he was also excited for the opportunity. He'd heard of Richard's father and knew he raised soybeans, a crop he wanted to learn more about.

He realized this might be the last summer Bill could do what he wanted. Hugh was looking for opportunities for Bill to do apprenticeships that would make him attractive to State when the time came to apply.

When Hugh picked Bill up a few days later, Bill couldn't stop talking about his new friend and the chance to fly.

"Well, I know learning to fly is a goal and a passion," Hugh said. "I guess it will be all right to spend the summer with Richard. And, if it's what you want, it's okay to work at the farm. I'd kind of like to see the place before you go, talk to Mr. Mitchell about what he's doing on the farm, get a feel for how good he is in that plane."

Bill felt sure his father would approve of Mr. Mitchell. They planned the trip to the farm in eastern North Carolina. Hugh told Bill to pack his suitcase for the summer because he had called Mr. Mitchell to ask if he could visit. He seemed only too happy to show off the land he was so proud of, and he wanted to pick Hugh's brain about what he was doing with his much larger property.

Since Hugh and Bill had been to Nags Head, they knew the land in the eastern part of the state was pretty flat. That made Hugh feel better about Bill learning to fly—no big hills or mountains to get in the way.

The whole Mitchell family greeted Hugh and Bill. Richard's sister, Belle, a redhead, wore a look of curiosity. Edward Mitchell was more than six feet tall and muscular. Mrs. Mitchell was also tall, and redheaded. Richard was in dungarees and grinning ear-to-ear.

"Come in, come in. Sherman here will take your luggage," he said, pointing to a Black man in work clothes. The house was large, with four bedrooms upstairs and one downstairs.

Edward pointed out a fancy chandelier in the dining room, but was most excited to show them the kitchen, which had all the modern conveniences.

Richard took Bill upstairs to the room they would share for

the summer, while Hugh was escorted to his room by Mrs. Mitchell. "Welcome to our home. I'm so glad Richard and Bill are friends. Bill has been a good influence on him," she said.

"Thank you, Mrs. Mitchell. I'm hoping this will be a good summer for them both," Hugh said.

They reconvened on the wide front porch with glasses of lemonade. Richard's little sister stayed in the kitchen with Mrs. Sherman, the cook.

The very first question Hugh asked was about the biplane. Who made it, how long had Mr. Mitchell had it, where did he learn to fly. How was the weather in the area.

Edward laughed. "I see your passions are similar to mine. Flight is the most amazing experience in the world. It's the transportation of the future. We'll go look at the plane directly, and you can talk to my mechanic, Irving."

Then the talk turned to crops and Richard and Bill tried not to roll their eyes. They wanted to see the plane. Bill knew that Mr. Mitchell was happy to talk about his soybean crop, as well as a small crop of peanuts. The soil in McNeill County was a little heavy for peanuts, Hugh thought, but they talked about ways to amend the soil and the prices the two crops fetched.

Mrs. Mitchell excused herself to check on Belle and supper.

Irving was in the building that housed the plane, getting it ready for flight.

A bandy-legged man with thinning hair, he seemed to always be in motion and Bill could tell he was immensely proud of the plane. The building also housed some of the farm equipment, and Edward explained that the whole farm would fall apart were it not for Irving.

"Now, if you young gentlemen wouldn't mind, I'm taking Mr. Henderson for a little tour of the area." Bill and Richard were visibly disappointed. "Don't worry boys, we have the rest of the summer ahead of us."

The plane was a thing of beauty in the sunlight. Bill fell in love immediately, his heart pounding as the engine spurted to life and the prop started spinning.

He could see his father smiling and laughing while Mr. Mitchell tugged at his leather helmet and placed goggles on his face.

They were off.

"Richard!!! I can't believe this is happening!"

"I've flown with him a few times. It's not like anything else on earth – because you're off the earth."

The plane gained speed and lifted off from the grassy airstrip.

"They'll be gone about an hour," I reckon, Irving said. "Let's start with your first lesson. You have to know why and how a plane works before you even set foot in it."

Irving had diagrams and drawings, tools, maps. Richard had heard some of it before, but a lot of it was new to Bill, and both young men were completely fascinated by what Irving was telling them.

When the plane returned, with a perfect landing, both men were smiling and laughing.

“Beautiful country here,” Hugh said. “Thanks for the tour and putting my mind at ease.

“Between Irving and myself, these boys are going to know everything about this plane. I’ll bet they can earn their licenses quickly. And I’m going to teach Bill everything I know about these crops. You understand that gentleman. Learning to fly is reward for learning to work.”

During the week, Bill and Richard worked in the fields and read about crop science and land management. Irving made sure they touched a part of the plane every other day, so they would understand what was going on when they were up in the air.

Edward realized that Bill was exceptionally good in science and understood a lot of what made certain crops more desirable in different areas. He hoped Richard would become more interested in the farm, too, because he wanted his son to take over one day.

Richard, of course, was more interested in flying. He worked hard on the farm, but he wasn’t sure yet if that’s where his future was. He had a lot to learn about so many things.

Every Saturday, he and Bill took turns in the plane, usually with Edward, because he was excited, but sometimes with Irving, who seemed like he could sprout wings and fly on his own, like he was the biplane.

Then came the Saturday Bill soloed.

Irving, Mr. Mitchell and Richard were standing by the airstrip when Bill landed and cut a chunk out of his shirttail — a pilot’s tradition. He was over the moon.

Richard soloed the next day, so the Mitchells planned a party to celebrate their accomplishment. It was almost time to go back to Woodberry Forest, so Edward Mitchell invited Hugh to join them. The plan was to let Richard start the party with a short flight, followed by Bill.

Bill couldn't have been happier. He liked learning about the science of growing crops, about the mechanics of flying.

The Mitchells had been good hosts and he and Richard got on well.

Richard told Bill he was thinking of becoming a pilot, instead of taking over the farm.

"Think of what the girls will say if I'm a pilot, instead of a farmer!"

"But your dad does more than farm," Bill said. "I'm not sure I want to work on our farm, either, but I owe something to my father. We could be pilots and land managers, couldn't we? I mean, you could fly over here and go other places to learn more. I want to talk Dad into buying an airplane because we have so many acres to look at."

Richard laughed. "You want it all, don't you?"

"Why not?"

When they went back to school, they told everyone about flying, and the girls they saw at mixers with Chatham Hall, a girl's boarding prep school, were impressed. Bill thought some of them didn't believe him, but he loved to talk about it.

When Bill learned to fly with Richard Mitchell, Hugh bought his son a used Piper Cub, by God! Bill and Hugh spent many a happy Sunday afternoon flying to the next county and back, surveying their property from the air. Whether from the air or on the ground, Hugh taught Bill to be a good steward of their land.

Since they'd both been bitten by the flying bug, Hugh and Bill built an airstrip on their vast property. Bill planned to expand the strip if he ever bought a larger plane.

Something told him he would.

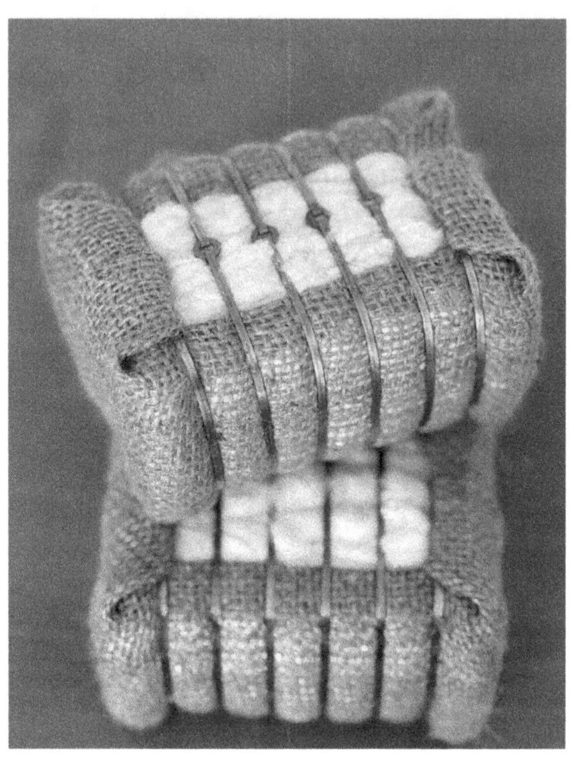

Hugh opens his own cotton brokerage firm

In 1940, Hugh took the little bit of money he had and started a cotton brokerage firm, buying and selling cotton, and dealing in cotton futures. He was well liked, he knew cotton futures, and he wasn't a brat. He had a fifth-grade education, but he was common-sense smart. He knew how to read and write, and boy, was he good at math.

He had an outgoing personality and was a true people person. Easy to get along with. He was in the right place at the right time as demand for raw materials skyrocketed after America got into WWII. He was so successful that Merrill Lynch Pierce Finner and Bean offered to put a complimentary ticker tape machine in his office. He took them up on the offer.

Hugh met Jake Brady early on in his career. They became fast friends. Jake was a managing partner at Merrill, but down-to-earth. Like Hugh, he'd been raised on a farm. He went to Carolina and earned a degree in business. He came into the firm as an apprentice, and he soon set his sights toward stock and commodity trading.

Hugh also dealt with Thompson McKinnon Auchincloss, another big investment brokerage firm. He invested with both groups, as well as Goodbody and Co. He did exceedingly well.

Each morning, Hugh got to the office early. His secretary had his black coffee and apple Danish ready. He had a sweet tooth, but that was his only daily indulgence. While he ate breakfast, he read the Greensboro Daily News, the Charlotte Observer, the Wall Street Journal, and the New York Times. He had two phones on his desk, one for local calls and one for long distance.

Hugh liked the look of a full cotton bale and had a friend build him a machine that bundled miniature ones which he handed out like business cards. They were a hit. Nobody else had anything like it.

His secretary, Betty Brinkley, had come to work with him when the mill closed. She'd pick up the newspapers from the post office every morning and drop off the outgoing mail on the way home each afternoon.

Betty's husband had been killed at Pearl Harbor. They had no children. She and Hugh got along well, despite their age difference. Betty probably would have married him had he asked. She carried a torch for him her whole life. But he never noticed — he never got over the death of his wife. But the two remained lifelong friends and co-workers.

The perfect couple

When Bill met the woman he would marry, he didn't even see the signs of trouble ahead.
Elizabeth Benson's family owned a cotton mill.

The Benson brothers had bet on a slow recovery in cotton mills across the South — so much so that they sold cotton futures short, putting up 5 percent of the value of the sales price when the contracts were due. The Benson family sold close to 1 million pounds of cotton at 20 cents per pound, expecting it to drop down to 5 or 10 cents per pound. For a while, it looked as if they were right in their speculation. They had put up everything they owned in this vision they had.

Then Hitler went on a march to conquer the world. Cotton went to 65 cents a pound at settlement time as Hitler invaded France. Militaries around the world bought up cotton to manufacture uniforms. As the price of cotton rose, the Benson brothers tried to get out but were locked in until the settlement date came. They were ruined.

They owed several million dollars and had put up the deed to the Benson Cotton Mills Co. as collateral. By early 1940, they were bankrupt. The mill fell into receivership, and the Bensons had to sell their homes.

Before all this happened, Bill had started dating Elizabeth. It was a small town, and they ran in the same circles. The bankruptcy had no effect on the love he had always felt for her. He knew the landscape had definitely changed, but she was beautiful and wild. Bill made the mistake of thinking he could tame her. He loved Elizabeth and wanted to marry her.

Hugh was adamantly opposed to his son's choice. He had seen her growing up, and there was just no other way to describe her but as a country club brat. Bill knew it, and so did his father. Elizabeth's father tried his best, but with no wife to help him, he couldn't manage such a willful child on his own. His wife had died early in their marriage.

Elizabeth and Bill had that in common. That shared sorrow was one of the things that drew them together. That's a deep bond that's hard to escape. Now, Elizabeth was a country club brat with no country club and no money. Bill's father couldn't see why in the hell he'd want to marry her.

But they say love is blind, right? In Bill's case, he learned it's also deaf, dumb, and stupid.

Elizabeth constantly clashed with her father, who eventually gave up trying to manage her. Against the wishes of both families, Bill and Elizabeth eloped on New Year's Day to South Carolina and returned home a married couple.

Bill and Elizabeth were the perfect couple — from the outside looking in. Bill's father survived the Great Depression. Bill was lucky to graduate from State College with a double major in agriculture and forestry management, and a minor in textiles. Naturally, he went to work with his father, starting out as a clerk, learning about the cotton business, step by step. He was a dedicated student and fast learner under his father's tutelage.

That was a good thing. Elizabeth got pregnant on their wedding night, the first of many challenges to their marriage.

Bob was born Oct. 1, 1940, and his sister, Elizabeth — they called her Liz — followed Dec. 7, 1941. What a day that turned out to be for the Henderson family. Even though the siblings were barely two years apart, they were never close. It haunted Bob throughout his life.

Entering WWII

It was no surprise to Hugh that Bill decided to go off to war just after the attack on Pearl Harbor. Elizabeth was unhappy with him. Even this early in the marriage, Bill had a feeling she'd always be unhappy. They had two young babies at home, but he couldn't shirk his patriotic duty. After all, he was named for a relative who went off to war at 14.

Elizabeth told him he was abandoning her if he went. Liz was only a few months old and a colicky baby. She cried all the time, often triggering Bob to cry. They didn't have quite enough money for the nanny Elizabeth desperately wanted. She begged Bill to get his father to pay for it, but Bill talked to Hugh and asked he not interfere. He thought children would knock some common sense into his wife. All it did was infuriate her. She often left Liz crying alone when she just couldn't stand it anymore.

As stubborn as she was, Bill was, too. He felt he wouldn't be a real man unless he served his country.

Things started out well enough. Bill enlisted in the Army Air Force, a branch that was headed to become a service all its own. Because he could fly, he pictured himself as a combat ace, maybe even flying civilian flights after the war was over, like his friend Richard.

He became a paratrooper, with five other Southerners under his command. Mark "Cotton" Ledford and Matthew "Bird Dog" Ledford were third-generation moonshiners from the North Carolina mountains. They were honest, hard-working men. Then there was Buck Wright and his twin brothers, Pete and Hoke. Buck was only 18 while the twins were a year younger. Their daddy had to sign for the younger boys, but they were determined to follow their brother — whom they loved but feared — into battle.

Buck's superiors from another division asked Bill to take him on. He was a paratrooper who had put a man's eye out in a bar fight. In the throes of war, there was no time for a court martial.

"I'll do it, but if he crosses me, I'll kill him," Bill said, and he made sure Buck knew it, too.

Bill's service ended when his right leg was hit by shrapnel from an exploded land mine in Italy. He was shipped home after a lengthy convalescent period, addicted to morphine, although he didn't realize it at the time. What he faced when he got home seemed even worse than nearly losing a leg — a wife who no longer loved him.

Don Juan

Elizabeth had had enough. While Bill was gone, she started seeing a country club playboy, leaving the children in the care of a young woman she met as a waitress at the club. Elizabeth was desperate for attention. Caring for children was not her role in life, she decided. They were wonderful when they were happy, sweet and totally devoted to her, but they were inconvenient, too.

When she decided her new man was a better catch than Bill, she had a friend fly her to Reno for one of those quickie divorces. Then she married the playboy and decided one child was more than enough, thank you very much, and left Bob with Bill. She took Liz, because she was a girl.

Bob moved with his father to The Retreat, a 2,000-acre home place his grandfather bought after Alcoa started gobbling up property for a reservoir. Hugh moved to one of the cabins on the property. He didn't need all that space and certainly didn't want to be in Bill and Bob's way. They needed some father-son bonding time.

Bob felt a little scared because his mother was gone, and he didn't understand she wasn't coming back.

When Bob got older, he started to understand more about

what had happened to his father. When his mother left, his father was still suffering from his war injury and hooked on morphine. That made Bob angry about his mother. As far as he was concerned, his father was a hero, and so was his grandfather.

Bill never called Elizabeth's second husband anything but "Don Juan." He didn't deserve to be called by his real name. Years later, he couldn't even remember the man's real name. Bob referred to him as Don Juan, too, not understanding what it meant, but thinking that was his real name.

They never had any contact.

Don Juan's family lost their money in the early 1930s, but he still retained his taste for the high life. He was an excellent golfer, an excellent dancer, and an excellent drinker.

Past that? Not much.

He'd somehow cheated his way out of entering service. Nobody in town was surprised. He had his pick of women at the club. He chose Bob's mother for his "one and only" — that's what he told her.

Don Juan saw the wealth that Hugh and Bill were able to accumulate and keep. He felt he could open a small office and do the same thing. He hired a secretary familiar with the cotton business, but only on a small scale. Bill figured that pretty young secretary did more than type for him.

He started making trades in cotton futures and was somewhat successful at the beginning. His confidence grew, not based on knowledge or research in the industry, but his gut feeling — a dangerous method.

Hugh and Bill sat back and watched. They could forecast the

inevitable, like seeing storm clouds gather on the horizon. And what dark, dark clouds they were. Sure enough, Bob's stepfather went a little too far, went on margin a little too deep, gave false financial statements to the brokerage house, and then the market turned down.

Meanwhile, Bob's father and grandfather had done their research, and had sold out of their positions by then. They parked their money in government bonds and waited until the market got back to where they hoped it needed to be. They'd done this many times before in unstable periods.

Elizabeth and Don Juan had a big party at their house the night he learned he'd been wiped out. He lost all his equity, his money, and his account with the brokerage house was closed. Not only had he lost his money and whatever money Elizabeth had, he owed the brokerage house a half-million dollars. He could not pay, borrow, or sell anything to come up with it.

They didn't even have enough cash to pay the help that night. They drank what liquor they had in the house, which was a considerable amount. He faked his way through the evening. Elizabeth was clueless. After the last guest left, she still did not know the straits they were in, and Don Juan wasn't about to tell her they were broke — and then some.

And so, he snuck into his study after she'd gone to her bedroom. He locked the door, pulled out a small-caliber gun, and shot himself in the head.

Elizabeth and the live-in handyman heard the shot. He broke the lock on the door to the study. They called an ambulance to take Don Juan to the hospital. After several hours, he was alive and breathing but not responsive.

Still, he lingered.

House of cards

Elizabeth often spoke to herself in the mirror of her vanity.

"Dear God, did he linger!" she said.

Over the next week, Elizabeth found out they were, in fact, broke, and would have to put the house on the market to cover the expenses to the brokerage house and the mounting hospital bills.

"Not the house!"

How could this have happened? Elizabeth thought her husband was a successful businessman. He always told her she was never to worry about his work, so she didn't.

Her life went on the way it always had, except for the fact there were no parties at the club because of the war. She had to make herself content with sitting by the pool with Liz or having lunch with friends who were equally bored by the situation in which they found themselves. They were all trophy wives, and their husbands were too old to serve.

"If only Bill hadn't gone to war," Elizabeth brooded. "There was no need for him to go. Something about duty to country and patriotism, blah, blah, blah. It always gave me a headache. Damn him for putting me in this position."

It never occurred to her that she played a large part in her own troubles.

Elizabeth was left with only one option. She called her former father-in-law, Hugh, and invited him over. Her plan was to beg him for money.

"I'll even be your mistress if you help me," she told him.

"The old goat declined," she yelled at her mirror later.

He told Elizabeth he'd put a small amount of money in a trust, which he would manage, to cover Liz's needs and education until she was 25, and do his best to find Elizabeth a job she was capable of doing.

"A job? Me? Are you out of your mind? You've got to be kidding!" she screamed at him as he walked to the front door. "You need to look after me, too. And you, you old bastard, I offered to look after you!"

Swallowing his disgust at the idea, he turned to leave.

Then he stopped, wheeled around, and looked her straight in the eye.

"Elizabeth, I never liked you. You know that. I tolerated you because of Bill, and my two grandchildren. Those days are over. Let me know what corner you're selling apples on. Have a nice day."

"You didn't mean for me to have a nice day. You were telling me to go to hell. Damn you," she shouted at the closed door.

Death of Don Juan

The night Don Juan shot himself, Hugh went to the hospital, along with Dr. Ben Brown, one of his best friends. He was a country doctor, a good man. They climbed the steps to the third floor to the playboy's room. Doc studied the chart at the foot of the bed.

"Doesn't look good, Hugh."

As the two of them walked down the hall a few minutes later, they passed Elizabeth going into his room. She shot daggers Hugh's way and kept going.

"Wait a minute, Doc. I want to hear what she says in that room," Hugh said.

The two of them quietly crept back and stood outside the room.

That woman unleashed a tirade on Don Juan, complaining about the mounting bills. Her words would have made a sailor blush. Doc and Hugh stared at each other, incredulous.

"You're so damned stupid! You can't even kill yourself right," Elizabeth snarled at him. "You used a small-caliber gun, you didn't know where to put it, and now you're lying here a vegetable. Damn you!"

Hugh turned to Doc and whispered, "Can you believe my son ever married this woman?"

They hightailed it out of there before she left the room.

Several days after that encounter — on Good Friday, no less — Elizabeth was seen taking flowers to her husband's room and closing the door. Somehow during her visit, Don Juan stopped breathing. She was never charged. There was no investigation. Don Juan had no family who came forward. There was no autopsy.

Elizabeth and Liz eventually moved to her family's vacation home in Blowing Rock in search of a fresh start. The house was the only thing spared in the financial debacle. In her new hometown, Elizabeth remarried again and again, using her country club charms. Each time was a disaster. She was a serial wife. With every husband and every failure, she drank more and more. Hugh heard updates from time to time from friends who owned mountain homes. It was like watching a train wreck in slow motion. For his granddaughter Liz's sake, Hugh wished there was something he could do.

In the end, there was nothing anyone could do.

Running 'shine

Through the years, Bill developed a close relationship with two other members of the paratrooper group he'd been in. Cotton and Bird Dog Ledford's daddy and granddaddy, Big Charlie and Little Charlie, had been arrested by the revenuers. They served time, then went right back to moonshining as soon as they were released.

They dug deeper into the woods, looking for clear streams with good water, a flat place to build the still and a way to get in and out without attracting attention.

They had a spring-fed branch in a wooded area that the revenuers never discovered. The rest of the family worked hard to keep the farm going. They grew tobacco and corn, and kept dairy cows, chickens and pigs for meat. They were only arrested when they were running 'shine – always the most dangerous part of the operation.

Bill ended up being the mastermind — their words, not his — behind the moonshine operation for Cotton and Bird Dog.

Bill hired a trustworthy attorney and a sterling accounting firm. He put his profits into The Retreat homeplace. Bill and his family were fortunate to have made quite a bit of money toward the end of the war with the cotton brokerage house. With the windfall, he bought some mom-and-pop stores and small service stations in the western part of the state.

You can't make moonshine without sugar — no matter how sweet your corn is. To ferment the grain, you must use yeast, and yeast feeds on sugar. Revenuers knew that. If someone bought 100 pounds of sugar, or 50, that was a sure sign of something going on.

Bill suggested running sugar through the stores he'd bought up near where the Ledfords lived, deep in the mountains.

They figured that the Ledfords required about eight different stores to buy their sugar. Once Bill's family owned them, nobody was suspicious. And if some local sheriff got too nosy, well, it was easy enough to change his mood with a little jar of happiness.

In order to get the sugar that Big Charlie needed, the grocery stores near Waynesville sold bags of sugar to 10 different companies owned by — you guessed it — Bill. Aunt Maude's Homemade Jams and Jellies were real products and were delicious. Since he owned the company that made jams and jellies, the revenuers never suspected that some of the sugar was being diverted to the Ledfords.

Bill was a legitimate businessman who also happened to be a disabled WWII veteran. In the eyes of the law, he was untouchable. And he was smart. He knew the law would be watching, so he had people looking back, trying to stay one or more steps ahead.

The jams and jellies were sold in jars with a cute picture of "Aunt Maude" on the label. Everybody thought there was a real Aunt Maude, but one day they threw a wig on Little Charlie and took his picture. It was pretty damn funny if you knew the inside joke. The jars, from pints to quarts, were also the source for the moonshiners' products, so again, it didn't arouse any suspicion.

As demand went up for the good moonshine, the third step in the process was to find a place to make it on a larger scale than the still in the woods.

When Cotton and Bird Dog got out of the service, Bill loaned them the money to buy a 2,000-acre cattle farm, producing milk for New River Dairy, Inc. — another one of Bill's companies. They pasteurized and bottled their own milk with equipment bought with a loan from Bill. The milk was sold through the little mom-and-pop grocery chain.

To wrap up the pretty package they'd created, from sugar to 'shine, Bill owned a small trucking company to transport the milk, jam, sugar, and so forth. Underneath the barns and milking parlors, the Ledfords built stills in proper rooms, not just holes in the ground or caves, but rooms with light and proper ventilation.

Once they were all set up, they sold their products — all of their products — at the mom-and-pop stores throughout western North Carolina and into eastern Tennessee. The moonshine was never dropped off at the same time or place. Big Charlie did what he did best — supervising the moonshine production on the farm.

Eventually, Bill decided to give stock in the company to Big Charlie and his boys. He kept 51 percent, while they divided the remaining 49 percent three ways. It was a good partnership for many years. Everybody was happy.

Hugh always told Bill not to toot his own horn. But Bill had developed this plan while lying in bed in northern England as he recovered from his war injuries. He liked Cotton and Bird Dog from the start. They were loyal and, surprisingly, they didn't drink at all because of the strict Baptist upbringing from their maternal grandmother. They learned early on that if they kept their wits about them, nobody could steal their moonshine or their profits, and the revenuers would not likely find them.

The boys' grandfathers and great-grandfathers had made enough mistakes. The brothers preferred to own a quality distillery, ahead of the times, which produced a smooth, safe drink. Moonshine was ready when it flowed into the jars. The brothers then learned a thing or two about whiskey, and what they could make on that — way more than 'shine. They invested in barrels to age the product and expand their market.

They learned about adding flavors to the corn liquor – the people especially liked cherry – cherry bounce had originated in England centuries back, and came across the ocean with the colonists.

They sold a helluva lot of moonshine. Their customers had Saturday night square dances and barn dances scattered through the hills. You could also find their corn liquor in just about every cabin in western North Carolina.

And it was the only whiskey ever served at The Retreat.

The mistake of hiring Buck

Buck Wright — another member of Bill's paratrooper group — married Hazel Norris in 1950 when she was 18. Per her parents' wishes, Buck waited for her to graduate from high school so they could marry. He turned 25 that year and figured it was high time he had a wife.

They met at an annual harvest dance hosted by the local grange. Hazel was 15 at the time — a natural, wholesome beauty — but her parents made her wait three years to marry. That was non-negotiable for Mr. and Mrs. Norris.

Buck could be charming when he wanted to, and boy, did he turn all his charm on Hazel. She was helpless to resist after that. He beat her for the first time on their honeymoon. After that, she could never have children.

Had Bill known, he would have killed him as soon as they returned to The Retreat.

Bill had hired Buck to be the caretaker when he came back from the war. He was thrilled to have a free place to live in exchange for working the acreage. Bill used "working" in the loosest sense of the word. He found out before long that Buck was lazy. Bill thought he should've known better. People asked him for years why he took up for Buck. Sure, he'd heard rumors about how he treated Hazel and his brothers. But Bill was so deep in a morphine haze then, he was sorry to admit, that he turned a blind eye. Hazel had no choice but to stay. Her parents died in an automobile crash not long after she married Buck. She, too, was an only child.

Another thing — Buck was the one who saved Bill's life when all that shrapnel shredded his leg, dragging him to safety. He owed Buck his life. How do you repay something like that?

In his more lucid moments, Bill knew on some level that

something was wrong. There was a low level of stress all around the farm, like a vibrating hum. It would take him years to figure out exactly how bad the problem was. Bill was ashamed of that for the rest of his life, especially because of how it eventually affected his son, Bob.

Buck's mistake

Buck was tolerable when he was sober. But he was mean as hell when he drank – which was often since the war. They all had seen things they never discussed. Ever. The Ledford boys put all their energy into growing their business. Bill's morphine addiction kept him just hazy enough that he didn't think about the war. Plus, he was so busy with his stores, dairy, jam production and trucking operation, it took all his concentration just to juggle all that and stay ahead of persistent revenuers.

For whatever reason, Buck seemed most affected. Maybe it was because being a soldier released some of the rage that lived inside him. Without that, the violence had nowhere to go, except towards those closest to him.

Once a month, Bill invited his poker buddies – mostly doctors but a few bankers thrown in for good measure – down to play cards at The Retreat. He had two cases of moonshine dropped off next to the gate. After playing cards a while, Bill would have to turn in early. It was time for his nightly morphine dose. It was the only way he could sleep. Hazel made snacks, and Buck was a half-ass gentleman, he heard from his buddies. He also helped himself to quart-sized jars of moonshine and hid them under his bed. Bill knew about this, of course, but there was no need to confront Buck.

But when Cotton and Bird Dog found out after Bill made an off-hand comment about it, they were mad as fire. They didn't want anybody cutting into Capt. Bill's stash, they said, even if he was a former Army Air Corps veteran. Buck was never their buddy, they resented him, and they could see right through him, even when Bill wanted to give Buck the benefit of the doubt. He was still indebted to Buck – whether anyone liked it or not.

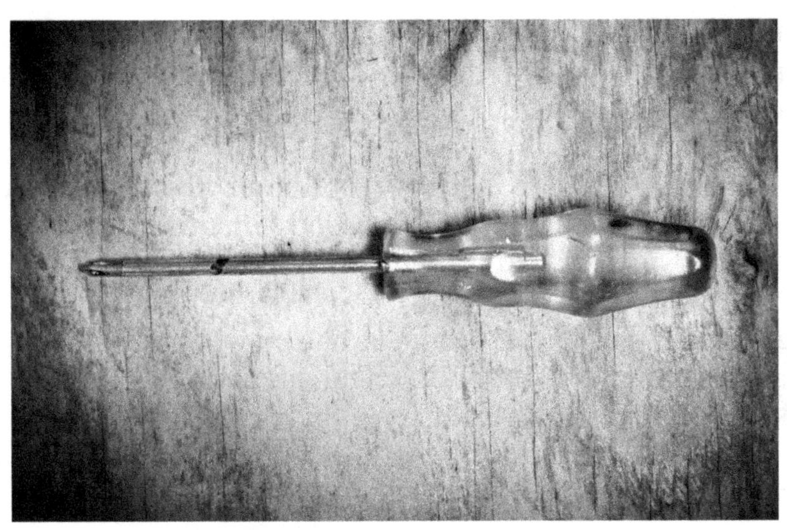

The night Buck died

Bob never forgot the afternoon Buck and Bill and Joe, Bill's favorite retriever, went hunting. Bob stayed back, parching peanuts with Hazel. He had turned 16 just the month before.

It was a cold November day. Hazel kept putting wood on the fire in the living room. The house still wasn't warm.

Hazel was attractive — when she didn't have a black eye. Which was more often than not. She told Bill her balance was off, that she fell a lot. He believed her, or at least took her at her word.

Bob kept noticing her as she bent to put wood on the fire. Over the past few months, he'd started having feelings he hadn't before. He knew it sounded horrible to feel that way about someone who raised him, but an instinct ignited in him.

Hazel turned around and caught Bob looking at her. She twirled a couple of times, giggling, and noticed he was aroused. Bob was embarrassed, his face turning red. Hazel went to touch his face and said, “It’s all right. I hate Buck as much as you do. Don’t worry about my relationship with him, because there isn’t one.”

Then she asked Bob to lock the front door, which they rarely did. She took him by the hand and led him upstairs to his bedroom. The door had no lock, but she gently closed it.

“Lie down and relax,” she said, as she slowly took off her dress and stood in front of Bob. Only in her mid-30s, she looked beautiful to the teen.

To him, she always was.

Gently, she kissed Bob’s face and neck. “Now take off your clothes and put them over there on the chair,” she said.

Although it had to be disappointing for Hazel, those next few moments for Bob were magic. Absolute magic.

“When you got into this bed, you were a boy. Now you’re a man.”

She kissed Bob on the lips once more. He thought, “Surely this is heaven on earth.”

Just then, they heard heavy footsteps on the porch. After hunting, Bill and Buck had gone to check the fences. Bill thought it would snow soon, and he wanted to be prepared. No matter what, he was always a good steward of the land he owned. Now they were stomping the dirt off their boots before they entered the kitchen — which would be any second.

Bob jumped up, dressed, and stumbled downstairs, falling into a chair beside the living room fireplace. Hazel stayed upstairs to dress in the hallway bathroom.

The back door flew open, and Buck's dark brown eyes bored into Bob.

"Boy, you better sit back from that fireplace. You look red as a beet."

If Buck only knew.

Or did he?

Bill was worn out. Hazel came in a few minutes later and helped him up to his bedroom, and he crumpled into his bed.

Bob stayed in the living room, getting himself together. His head was spinning. That's when he realized that Buck was in a bad way. Drunk. Very drunk. He had been drinking to keep warm the whole time they were out.

That's when Bob knew Buck was pure evil. It oozed from his pores.

After the first night Bob saw Buck attack Hazel, he started keeping a Boy Scout knife in his right front pants pocket. He patted his jeans to make sure it was there, but realized he'd left it in his uniform pocket from the Boy Scout troop meeting the night before. It was in the washroom in the outdoor kitchen, and he couldn't get there except by going through the indoor kitchen.

"Dammit," Bob cursed. He had an ominous feeling that things were going to go from bad to worse. He was right. From the kitchen, he could hear Buck slapping Hazel.

"That's right, bitch, cry," he shouted. "If you were a real woman, you could have had kids. I wasted my time on you."

Bob cowered behind the sofa, frozen. He didn't know what to

do. He felt like a child. He used to hide behind that same sofa when he and Buck played hide and go seek, the only positive memory he had of him.

Hazel fell to the floor, crying. Bob listened until he couldn't handle it anymore.

He suddenly realized he had a weapon after all.
Bob reached into his back pocket and pulled out a Phillips head screwdriver he'd been using earlier in the afternoon while tinkering with the old tractor. It might not hurt Buck much, but he could try.

Before he could change his mind, he charged up behind Buck at full speed and plunged the screwdriver into his upper left shoulder with all his might. He did it twice more before even realizing what he was doing.

Buck whirled around in agony and stared at Bob.

"You! You!" was all he could manage, blood spurting from his miserable body.

He fell to the ground and started to gasp, blood pouring from the wound.
"What have you done?" Hazel screamed.

"Hazel, I couldn't take it anymore. I had to do it," Bob said.

Buck began vomiting blood and started to tremble and shake.

Bob was trembling, too. Buck was bleeding to death, his blood thinned by the alcohol.

Time slowed down.

"What have I done?" Bob thought.

It was all too much for his young mind to comprehend.

Buck lay on the floor, the life oozing out of him.

Hazel bent down to try to get a pulse, but Bob stopped her. Nobody needed to touch him. He knew that. With the blood oozing from his wounds, his pulse had to be faint.

Bob put the screwdriver back in his pocket and looked at Hazel. She looked back. They looked down at the dying Buck and stood there, motionless. It was only later they understood they were in a state of shock. Thankfully, it didn't take long for him to die. Bob had hit a main artery to his black heart. He got a quilt out of the downstairs linen closet and put it around Hazel. Then he got a drop cloth and covered Buck. He didn't want to see that contorted face one second longer.

"We've got to go get this blood off us," Hazel said.

They went to the outdoor kitchen and rinsed their hands. It was cold, so they worked fast. When they got back to the house, Hazel told Bob to strip.

He wondered what she meant until he looked down at his plaid shirt and jeans, which were covered in blood. He did as she said, then went up to change.

By the time he went back downstairs, she'd put on a clean dress from the washroom, and everything was in the washing machine.

Hazel and Bob sat in the living room in front of the fire for a long time — scared, numbed, relieved. So many feelings racing through their minds.

After a while, they looked at each other.

"What now?" Bob asked Hazel.

"We can't sit here all night. We need help."

"But who?"

"Your dad."

"My dad? My God, Hazel, what can he do? He's upstairs passed out on morphine."

Hazel didn't answer. She went upstairs and was gone for what seemed like hours. She said later it was about 30 minutes.

Hazel and Bill came downstairs. He was dressed, freshly showered and shaved. His hair was combed neatly into place. He was a completely different man than he'd been earlier that evening.

"Bob, come over here," he said, enveloping his son in a bear hug, tears in his eyes. "Hazel told me what's been going on and what happened tonight. Both of you need to gird yourselves. This needs to be handled so neither of you is tied to it."

He cleared his throat, and his voice was calm and steady. "I've called Cotton and Bird Dog, and they're on their way. You all are not to worry. I will handle this. I should have handled Buck a long time ago. Hazel, Bob, I am so sorry."

He gently kissed Hazel on the cheek, left the room, stopped in the kitchen briefly to make sure that Buck was indeed dead, and went into his study alone, closing the door behind him. Bob couldn't believe it. He was on top of his game, in charge of the situation. He moved with purpose for the first time since his injury in the war. He was barely limping. A calm came over Bob. As scared as he was, he felt good about his father, and how he would take care of Hazel and him.

"Hazel, what in the world can Dad do? I killed Buck! I'm going to prison! I'm going to the gas chamber!"

"Don't get ahead of yourself. Leave this to your father. He said you are not to worry."

Hazel spoke with conviction. Maybe there was hope after all.

Bob was only a kid. He didn't know how any of this worked. He only knew right from wrong. His world back then was black and white — no shades of gray.

He'd always had the feeling that his father could call Cotton and Bird Dog any time, day or night, and they would come. Sure enough, they arrived close to midnight.

Cotton, Bird Dog, and Bill took Buck's body out to the shed. They dressed him in fishing clothes which Hazel had fetched from their cabin, along with bib waders, a couple of fishing rods, and a tackle box full of lures and fishing line. They put two empty quart jars in the tackle box.

They loaded Buck's body and a small ax into a Jon boat. Cotton and Bird Dog took Buck out. Bill and Bob followed in their larger motorboat. They were all bundled against the cold. Hazel stayed back at the main house. She'd had enough trauma for one night.

A quarter moon guided them. Nobody else was around. It was dark, but Bill knew exactly where they were going. They trolled until they found the stump where Bill fished for crappie in the summertime.

Cotton joined Bill and Bob in their boat while Bird Dog knocked a hole in the front of the Jon boat with the ax. Before he did that, he jumped in the water, and working quickly, unspooled some fishing line around the stump.

Bird Dog then got into the motorboat, wrapping up in blankets they'd brought along expressly for that purpose. The four of them watched the Jon boat sink, Buck's body in it. No one said anything.

The four of them got back to The Retreat less than two hours later. They hadn't seen anyone coming or going. It was too damn cold. Bill said he'd call the sheriff around lunchtime. When Buck went out fishing, he was always home by dark.

This time, he wouldn't come home.

Bob went up to bed and slept without dreams. Bill talked to Cotton and Bird Dog for a while in his study. He invited them to spend the night, but they declined. They had to supervise the milkers who would arrive in just a couple short hours. Bill cautioned them to be careful on the way home and obey the speed limit. They arrived without incident, and all were finally free of the violent Buck.

The coroner

Lucy Athena Burdette was a firecracker. She grew up on her grandparents' farm. Her grandfather, Isaiah, was a lifelong friend of Bob's grandfather. In fact, Hugh and Isaiah, a Black boy, were playmates, and Hugh later deeded land to Isaiah to farm. This was unheard of during segregation, but Hugh was a man who did what was right. And he was a man who did what he wanted.

Add to that the fact that Isaiah — who couldn't swim — saved Hugh from drowning in a flash flood when they were youngsters. That cemented their friendship for the rest of their lives. As far as Hugh was concerned, they were equals. And if Hugh Henderson said something, he meant it. His word was his bond. No other White man in the county questioned him — or Isaiah Burdette, for that matter.

That was the kind of world — or privilege, if you will — into which Lucy Athena was born.

Standing 6 feet tall by the time she entered the segregated

high school, Lucy Athena soon became a star on the women's basketball team. White fans and college coaches alike came to see her play, although very few colleges had women's teams.

She also happened to make a perfect score on the SAT and she ended up with a scholarship to Oberlin College in Ohio. She worked hard there in an atmosphere which was still racially charged, but more accepting than any Ivy League school. But she was determined to get the best education possible, and she was ready to fight for it.

She applied to Yale, which had accepted only a few Black women into its medical school, and they were impressed enough with her grades and recommendations, along with a passionate essay about the future of women in medicine that they offered her a full scholarship.

It would not be until 1969 that Yale University accepted female students, so Lucy Athena was on the cutting edge.

Although a women's basketball team was still decades away, she was occasionally invited to scrimmage with the men at Oberlin. She was that good. She got a kick out of that. The men, not so much, but she quickly earned their respect on and off the court.

After Yale, Lucy Athena had several choice offers, mostly in large cities with large Black populations.
But she didn't want to be pigeonholed that way. She had learned with and competed against White men and women and decided her place in the world could be like anyone else's.

Instead, she decided to come home to McNeill County. She'd heard the county coroner's job was open. Ol' Doc Brown had finally kicked the bucket, and Lucy Athena, who had been fascinated by the dissection of cadavers in med school, wanted the job.

A few things worked in her favor. Even though she was Black, everyone in the county remembered her exploits on the basketball court. Who doesn't love a phenomenal athlete? She was a sports legend in McNeill County.

She'd graduated first in her high school class, first in her college class, and third in her med school class. The people of McNeill County knew they couldn't turn down that kind of expertise. Also, Hugh had run for county commissioner on a whim and was elected.

That was when the county votes ran blue, and the whole board was made up of Democrats. Civil rights hadn't come to the forefront yet, but the commissioners knew change was on the way. Why not be leaders?

Hugh made the motion, and the commissioners voted unanimously to elect Lucy Athena. The news made headlines all over the South. The sheriff and Hugh were close friends, so Lucy Athena's transition to her new job was smooth. She never had any trouble. And you couldn't get to the Burdette farm without going through the Henderson right-of-way. Not even the bravest Klansman had a taste for that.

Lucy Athena was a hard worker, and then some. She knew her material and did her job well. When she was doing an autopsy, color of skin did not matter. She quickly developed a rapport with the sheriff, the police chief, and the hospital's chief executive officer.

So it was that one morning in the spring of 1957 that Buck's body — which had been in the water for months by then — showed up on her stainless-steel table in the coroner's office.

Lucy Athena pulled on her custom-made, extra-long gown, her gloves, her cap, her goggles, and got to work.

First, she made note of the weight of the body — what was left of it — and any other pertinent information she thought would be helpful. There were no marks on the front of the body, save for a few punctures on his left shoulder. That jibed with what the fisherman who found him had reported.

Buck had presumably gone out fishing, got drunk and fell in the water, tangling himself in fishing line and getting caught in the submerged tree stump that was a favorite spot for many fishermen out in the county.

The tree stump could certainly account for those puncture marks. It seemed to her, though, that a man of Buck's size and physical condition could easily fight off some tangled fishing line. However, counting back a few months, Lucy Athena realized that the combination of the brutal cold of the air and water and the effects of the moonshine — he'd been found near two broken and corroded quart jars wedged in the boat, after all — could have taken him down right away.

Lucy Athena made these notes and pondered a few minutes before she turned over the body. She never rushed an autopsy.

Her eyes widened behind her goggles.

The cold water had preserved Buck's body well enough that she could make out the three separate wounds around his left shoulder blade. Not the kind of wounds a tree stump would make, after all. No, these were deliberate and close together, as if someone had done it quickly and violently.

Lucy Athena put down her pen and clipboard, pushed her goggles on her forehead, and thought some more.

The shape of the wounds reminded her of something, but what? She took her time, because she knew the answer would come to her. She also realized this wasn't a drunken accident.

It was a murder.

Lucy Athena looked over the rest of the body, this information percolating in the back of her mind. Nope, no other wounds, save for the usual damage you'd expect on a body that had been in the water for months.

Lucy Athena kept working and taking notes, efficient as always. After a while, she looked up at the clock. Noon already. Time for her lunch break. She took off her gear, carefully washed up, then went to the break room, pulling her lunchbox from the fridge. She moved gracefully, like a runway model.

She sat down at the card table that had belonged to Doc Brown's wife during her Canasta-playing days, opened her granddad's old metal lunchbox and took out her turkey sandwich and apple. She also had a thermos of chicken noodle soup. It was the same lunch her grandmother had packed for her every day she was in elementary school. Lucy Athena was a creature of habit.

She sat in the peace and quiet of the morgue, slowly chewing her sandwich, lost in thought. In a few minutes, she picked up the other half. Then the light bulb she had been waiting for went off. She carefully wrapped the half sandwich back in foil, grabbed her keys, and sprinted to the parking lot.

She ran to the back of her Impala and unlocked the trunk. The only thing in there was a shiny red toolbox. Her grandfather insisted that Lucy Athena keep it with her at all times. She knew how to change a tire — her granddaddy had made sure of that before she learned to drive — but she might need other tools, too, he reasoned. She made a mental note to thank her grandfather when she got home from work that evening, then hurried back to the morgue.

Once gowned up and back at Buck's side, Lucy carefully opened her toolbox and pulled out a Phillips-head screwdriver, placing it near but not touching the wound.

"Perfect fit. Dammit," she said softly.

The proximity of the lake to The Retreat made her uncomfortable. It followed that someone in the Henderson family or estate was involved in Buck's killing.

Lucy Athena immediately crossed Hugh off her short list. Hugh was getting on in years and while his health was fine, she doubted he'd have the strength to inflict such angry and ragged wounds.

Hugh's son Bill was Lucy Athena's height — around 6 feet. Or at least that's what he was before his leg injury. The limp from his war wound could affect the trajectory of the weapon. It would've been off.

Hazel wouldn't have the strength to do it, either. Not since Buck had been beating her for years. Everyone in town knew about that. Everyone, it seemed, but Bill. Buck's brothers were too afraid of him to fight back, from what she'd heard. Who else could have done it?

Lucy Athena suddenly felt sick to her stomach. She realized that Bob Henderson was the only person left on her list. He was tall and gangly, but with the right amount of adrenaline …

Lucy Athena thought and thought until she could think no

more. The sheriff had done no investigation, because it was Buck, whose reputation for violence was known throughout the county. And it was on Henderson property; the Henderson's were pillars of the community. Plus, the sheriff was relieved Buck was gone – he'd been nothing but trouble, and everyone knew he abused poor Hazel.

She took the toolbox and screwdriver and went back to the break room. Luckily, her assistant was out sick. She was working alone today. She finished her lunch, and then did something that she'd never done before and would never do again.

She came back into the exam area and carefully sewed up the body, including her cuts from the autopsy and the ragged wounds from the screwdriver. She owed Buck that. At all times, she was respectful of the dead — even if they weren't respectful of others in life.

When she was done with her task, she picked up her clipboard. She took off all the papers, folded them neatly, and put them in the bottom of her toolbox. As soon as she got home that evening, the papers would be reduced to ash in her grandfather's fire barrel. She'd make sure of that.

Next, she got out another set of forms and filled them out, writing down exactly what the fisherman and sheriff's deputy had suspected — that Buck had gone out fishing late that night, got drunk, fell in the water. The alcohol kept him from waking and struggling. The fishing line simply wrapped itself around his body when he sank into the dark, cold depths.

Case closed.

When Lucy Athena completed her paperwork, she called her cousin Buddy over at Roselle's, the Black funeral home. No one had come to claim Buck's body, not Hazel, not his brothers, so it didn't matter which funeral home did the honors. Roselle's would bill the county, and the funeral director, Moses Roselle, would happily accept the extra money.

When Buddy arrived in the next hour — it was a slow day at the funeral home and he'd just finished his lunch — Lucy Athena told him that nobody claimed Buck's body, and the Hendersons didn't want the expense of burying him. Another light bulb went off. In medical school, when cadavers had no one to claim them, the bodies were cremated.

Could that be a possibility for Buck?

Instinctively, Lucy Athena knew she had to get rid of the body as soon as possible. So, she asked Buddy where the body could be cremated. He looked surprised, but said the nearest city was either Charlotte or Greensboro. She told Buddy to take Buck's body to Roselle's and wait for her call with further instructions. Buddy did as he was told. Nobody in the Burdette family ever questioned Lucy Athena, or their patriarch Isaiah, for that matter.

Lucy Athena closed her office for the day — she had no other cases — and, although she dreaded it, drove straight out to The Retreat. Bill was glad to see her, but his smile faded when he saw the somber look on her face — and the fact she was carrying her shiny red toolbox. To him, it was a bright harbinger of doom.

"Bill, may we speak privately?"

"Of course, Lucy Athena. Come into my study."

The study was just to the left of the front door. Everyone else was out. It was still fairly early in the afternoon. Hazel hadn't come up to fix dinner yet, and Bob was at baseball practice.

"I'll get right to the point," Lucy Athena said, once she'd settled her frame into a comfortable club chair. "Buck was murdered."

"I know."

"And I know who did it."

"So do I."

Lucy Athena kept her poker face and continued.

"That's why I filled out the paperwork for an accidental death. Buck was drunk, fell in the water, and never woke up. Case closed."

She paused for a moment, gathering herself. She knew the next thing she said could mean she'd lose her license, everything she'd worked for.

"I will never do this again," she said, looking steadily at Bill. "Do we understand one another?"

Bill looked at her for a long while, too. He knew then and there that Lucy Athena would have a successful career as county coroner — maybe even elected office after that.

"Yes, Lucy. Yes, we do. And thank you. From the bottom of my heart."

"Well, then," Lucy Athena said, clearing her throat. "I'll show myself out."

"You send my best to your granddaddy."

Lucy Athena nodded once, then was gone. She was eager to get home to her grandparents for supper. She wanted to forget what she had seen, and her grandmother was making chicken and dumplings, her favorite. If ever there were a time for comforting and forgetting, this was it.

Bill sat at his desk for a long, long time, trying to calm his racing heart, breathing sighs of relief. Lucy Athena was not the only one who had perfected a poker face.

Once Bill's breathing returned to normal, he opened his desk drawer and reached all the way to the back. There was the Phillips head screwdriver that had done so much damage. That fateful night, Hazel had scrubbed it with hot soapy water, ammonia, and Bar Keepers Friend. There was no way it could ever be traced back to Bob. Bill and Hazel would carry that secret to their graves. The screwdriver would remain in the drawer as long as the family owned the house.

Bill never told anyone about the coroner's visit — not Bob, not Hazel.

Lucy Athena was as good as her word. It was a small county, but the two of them never crossed paths again in a professional setting. Roselle's arranged for cremation at a Charlotte facility where the ashes would be stored for a time, then properly disposed. The anonymous cash payment was never recorded.

Inflation hits

The Korean War started in the early 1950s. The cotton market popped again from 1949 to 1951. During that war, there were expectations of a third world war. At that point, Hugh got heavily involved in cotton futures once again. In 1952, he saw those futures weakening and sold off all his holdings. The previous years were profitable, giving him additional funds to buy more land. There was a window when no one knew when the war was going to end — but they did know it was the last hoorah for the cotton market.

In the late 1960s, Vietnam was going crazy. Inflation came into the picture. Nobody knew what that word even meant until then. Commodities went wild — upward with inflation. Jake Brady's son Jake Jr., now Bill's broker, urged him to invest in sugar, soybeans, wheat and corn. Bill thought of his old Woodberry classmate, Richard, and his soybean farm.

Bill stayed out of the cotton market as it had run its course, holding some commodities and trading up on others.
In 1974, with inflation running rampant throughout the world and commodities at all-time highs, Bill said to Hugo, "Let's get out. We've got huge profits. Let's don't be greedy. Let's put my money in land, certificates of deposit, and conservative blue-chip stocks."

Jake Jr. agreed, and Bill got a good night's sleep, at peace with his decision.

Time proved him right.

Photo by Sean Meyers Photography

A new farm manager

After Buck's demise, Bill realized he'd have to hire someone else to take over the management of the farm. Buck had taken a lot of shortcuts with the crops and equipment. That's not something you can sustain long term. Bill liked and trusted Pete and Hoke, but neither of them was interested in the job. They were hard workers, and they always did what they were asked. They also didn't have a whole lot of schooling, but they didn't want Bill to know that, even though he'd figured it out. It was a difficult decision for him to make. He'd been on morphine for so long, he'd lost contact with many business associates.

Buck's death turned out to be a godsend to Bill. To protect his son, he had to come back into reality and quickly. And to retake control of his property, he had to focus. Every day, he felt more like his former self. Most of Bill's poker buddies were doctors, so they explained to him how he could wean himself off the morphine safely over time and not suffer withdrawal.

He might have pushed it a little bit, but it was a challenge, and Bill was good at rising up to meet challenges. Once he was off the morphine, it was over. Bill was a different man.

Fortunately, those poker buddies had his implicit trust. The Hendersons had one of the largest farms in the county, and management was a big job. Bill thought he could trust Buck but ended up being wrong. This time, he wanted to make a better decision, so he looked to them for advice. He needed someone trustworthy, someone who knew the inner workings of a large farm. The family started interviewing candidates with agricultural experience and contacted N.C. State for a list of names.

They ended up with a young man named Kent James. His resume and personality impressed them. Before long, Kent became part of the family.

Kent came to work during summers as part of a work-study program through N.C. State. The family liked him and vice versa. Bill knew he would be the man who could eventually oversee the farm. Kent graduated with a double major in agriculture and forestry management. Bill then bought a 10-acre farm next door. He told Kent that after five years if everything worked out with his job, he would sell the land to him. He agreed. At the end of the five-year period, Bill liked Kent so much that he sold the land to him for half its worth and financed it at zero percent interest.

As other adjacent land became available, they bought it to put it in forestry. Bill and his father ultimately doubled the size of The Retreat to 2,000 acres. It was rewarding to conserve the land.

How lives changed

As Bob's life changed completely after the night Buck died, Bill's would change not long after.

In what seemed like no time, Bill was back to his old self, hunting and fishing and walking on The Retreat property with his dog Joe, regaining his stamina. He was tired of wallowing in his misery. He wanted his life back. Bob's grandfather was getting older, and Bill wanted to be there for him. Things in his life were getting back on track.

With Buck dead, Bob assumed he and Hazel could be together. They had to be careful, though, since Bob was living under Bill's roof. They made it work for several months, meeting at her cabin whenever Bill went into town to the office.

Bob knew his father would probably find out one day, but he was too obsessed with Hazel to care. Hazel seemed to take an interest in him, too. Or so Bob thought. Maybe she was in mourning for Buck, and this was her way of coping. But Bob was just a kid. He didn't care, as long as he could be with her. Bob was crazy in love.

Then one day, Bill came home early and started looking for Bob. The boat was at the dock, and the dogs were in their kennels. There was only one other place Bob could be, and it didn't take Bill long to suss it out. To his credit, he did not come down to the cabin but called Bob into his study after dinner. Hazel had gone home, so she didn't overhear the conversation. He told Bob he was planning to send him to his alma mater, Woodberry Forest, for his last two years of high school to better prepare him for college. Bob was on track to be valedictorian of his high school class, but Bill knew his son could be a better student if he were more challenged academically. Bob would come home for holidays and summer break.

Bob knew what his father was doing. He didn't like it at first, because he'd be away from Hazel. But he'd never disobeyed his father. Bill didn't say a word about Hazel and neither did Bob.

Obedient to his father, and with some excitement at a change, Bob went to Woodberry at the start of his junior year. Before long, he met some guys who would become lifelong friends. That's also where he developed his interest in biology and zoology and started taking all the science classes he could. It all came so easy.

Bill had always assumed Bob would go into business with him, but being at Woodberry opened Bob's eyes to other career possibilities. He started dreaming of being a doctor, and his teachers told him that with his stellar grades, that dream could become a reality if he worked hard. He kept his head down and took his studies seriously.

Bob had promised Hazel when he left home that he would write her once a week, but he never did because of the rigorous academic schedule. He hoped she'd understand, and after a while, the need was not so sharp. Bob often went to social events with Chatham Hall, a nearby girls' boarding school, and he was getting to know girls his age. It wasn't that they were better than Hazel. They were just different, and Bob came to realize that was okay.

Deep down, Bob knew a permanent relationship with Hazel was out of the question. Still, it hurt when he came home that Christmas and saw her favorite robe in his father's bathroom. He wasn't snooping. He had left his aftershave at school — they used the same brand — and needed to splash some on his face. Bob never said anything to his father about it. He figured that once he was out of the house, what happened there was his father's business. He wasn't even angry, because he knew that Hazel and his father had been good friends over the years. Bob understood that he and Hazel had no future, and he didn't want to upset his father because he had fought so hard to get well. Bill was Bob's hero and always would be. There would be other women for Bob.

How Hazel's life changed

After Bob left for Woodberry in the fall of 1956, another tragedy struck the family.

Elizabeth Henderson had taken Liz and moved permanently to Blowing Rock. Mutual friends told Bill how bad her drinking had gotten. Bill didn't care about Elizabeth, but he did care about his daughter. He certainly didn't want Liz in the car when Elizabeth was driving, but that's what happened. Elizabeth was such a control freak that she wouldn't turn the wheel over to Liz even when she should have. Liz had learned to drive years before in the country club neighborhood. All parents did it back then.

Late one rainy afternoon, the duo left the club after Elizabeth's weekly bridge game. There had been talk among the ladies at the club about rescinding Elizabeth's bridge group membership, as she became more and more obnoxious with every vodka tonic. She had been a damned good player before the booze took over.

Unfortunately, Elizabeth overheard two of the players gossiping about her when she was powdering her nose in the locker room. Incensed, she grabbed Liz — a quiet girl who always hung out in the ladies' lounge with her nose in a book because she had zero interest in bridge — and told her it was time to leave. Liz knew she should have taken her mother's keys, but she knew her mother would ignore her if she said anything. Ever the obedient daughter, she got in the car with her mother.

On the final curve before their driveway, Elizabeth's Jaguar struck a tree. She was killed instantly, and Liz was pinned in for an hour, her legs crushed.

Bill got the call that night. Bob was home for fall break, and they left for Blowing Rock immediately. Bill had Liz transferred to McNeill County Hospital, since it was larger and more capable of treating her injuries. She stayed in the hospital for six weeks, then Bill brought her to The Retreat for her convalescence. Her recovery would be long, but her prognosis was good, according to her doctors.

“Daddy, I missed you so much. I tried, I really tried, but she just wouldn’t let me help her,” Liz kept saying to Bill.

“Honey, you did nothing wrong. Your mother had a problem that she couldn’t face on her own, and she never would accept help that was offered to her,” Bill said. “We’re going to be a family again, you and Bob and me. We’re going to take care of you.”

Bill, Bob, and Hazel did their best to cater to Liz’s every need. Bob arranged to take the rest of the semester off — his grades were high, and his teachers mailed his assignments to him — and sat by her bedside every afternoon, reading to her from their favorite classic novels. A love of reading was the one thing they had in common. During that month, they got to know each other as young adults. Liz wasn’t the spoiled brat Bob assumed she’d be. She had to take responsibility and grow up fast as their mother’s alcoholism became more apparent.

“Liz, I feel sorry for all you had to put up with,” Bob said one day when they were reading “Great Expectations.”

“Being with you now helps so much, Bob. I never imagined we could really be like brother and sister. Mother did so much to keep us apart. It was like she threw away everything about our family, even her memories.”

Bob swore to himself he would never tell Liz about the horrible thing that happened with Buck. It was a burden he was still trying to bury. The others involved never mentioned it. It was a nightmare that had been gradually fading as time passed.

Bill embraced this second chance with his daughter. He'd take her wheelchair out on the porch when the weather was good. He told her about Hugh and The Retreat and how he would take her over every square inch of the property when she was well. Liz had been too young to remember any of it.

Hazel was an absolute angel when it came to taking care of Liz. Bill didn't know what he would have done without her. There were personal needs Liz preferred a woman take care of, and she was glad for Hazel's help. The two women became close. Hazel had long mourned the fact that she'd never been able to have children. Taking care of Liz satisfied her maternal longing and resurrected a high school dream she had of becoming a nurse one day. Her marriage to Buck had stripped her of all her dreams, but now she felt some hope. She decided she'd get up the nerve to ask Bill to send her to nursing school. She felt sure he would say yes. She wouldn't say a word until Liz was completely well. She hoped Liz would stay on at The Retreat, as the family had finally been reunited. It was a joyous Christmas, but the reunion would not last.

The family woke up on New Year's Day 1957 to discover that Liz had died in the night. Doc Brown's son, Dwight, came when Bill called. He said Liz had likely thrown a blood clot.

"She never knew what hit her," Dwight assured Bill, his hand resting on the older man's shoulder. "Take comfort in the joy she had these last couple of months. You did everything you could, Bill."

Bob was devastated that he'd lost the sister he was just getting to know. He still hadn't worked out how he felt about losing the mother who had basically abandoned him. But he hardly knew her. All she was to him was one bad decision, one awful problem after another.

The family buried Liz on the property, under the spread of a large oak tree that Bill had chosen for his own resting place.

One step at a time

Bob went back to Woodberry Forest after his sister's funeral, but he was much changed. Not only had he killed a man at 16, but he'd since lost a mother he hardly knew, and a sister he was just learning to love. It left a strange empty place in his heart. He didn't understand what grief was, and there really wasn't anyone to help him. You just didn't talk about these things with your friends or teachers.

Bob tried to be like his father, stoic and strong. He understood the expectations on him. That was clear enough. He did what his father had done after his war injury and after Buck's death. He carried on. He focused on his schoolwork.

He dreamed of going to Duke University, especially since Hazel was there and because he'd pretty much made up his mind that he wanted to be a physician. Once he was accepted to the school, he wrote to Hazel, who sent him a polite note of congratulations. She wished him well. Bob knew they would never be together, but he still wanted to impress her.

Bob visited his father every chance he got when he was home from Duke. When he told him he wanted to be a doctor instead of going into the cotton brokerage business, he said, "I can't blame you for that. This industry is changing. We were in it early enough to get a good living out of it and make some good investments which are keeping us in good shape. But the industry itself is changing."

A month after the funeral, when everything had been settled, Hazel approached Bill about going to nursing school. Although they had kept each other warm on lonely nights, both of them realized it was a relationship of mutual comfort and deep friendship. It was built on trust and shared secrets.

"Bill, I've been thinking about this a long time, and ever since Miss Liz, God rest her soul, was with us, I've been thinking again I'd like to train to be a nurse."

"I think that's a terrific idea," Bill told her. "You did such outstanding work with Liz. You're a natural."

She hugged him and whispered, "Thank you" over and over. She could imagine a new future with this opportunity.

Hazel applied to Watts School of Nursing in Durham. She sent in her high school transcript and took the pre-test. She was accepted immediately and moved to Durham to work and save money before she started school in the fall. Bill insisted on paying for her apartment, but Hazel wanted to pay for her other expenses. They spent one last romantic night together — Bill made sure of it — and then he took Hazel to the train station the next morning. She carried all her belongings in one large suitcase and a train case. It was a bittersweet goodbye as they hugged one last time before she left Magnolia train station headed to Durham. Bill watched her train until it slowly rounded the curve.

The letter

Hazel wrote Bill as frequently as she could, which was a challenge given her difficult schedule. Bill was as proud of her as he could be and told her so when he wrote.

Dearest Bill,

I can't say thank you often enough. The training is hard, but I love every minute of it. I almost feel as if this is who I was meant to be. After all you have done for me, you and your father and Bob, I want you to be proud of me and think about me once in a while. I study every chance I get and will be a good nurse.

Love,
Hazel

Bill was not really a letter writer, but he'd send short, encouraging notes to her when she wrote.
As the months and then years passed, Hazel's letters became less frequent. Bill didn't think anything of it. He figured it was because she was so busy with classes, then with her work as a nurse at Duke Hospital.

Then came the letter, arriving right after her annual Christmas card.

Dec. 20, 1961

Dearest Bill,

I'm sorry I haven't written in a while. My work has been going well. I so enjoyed all the rotations I did at Watts before being hired on the psychiatric floor at Duke. It is difficult work, but interesting and fulfilling. The psychiatry rotation was my favorite.

The biggest reason I'm writing is that I've met someone. He is a psychiatrist on the faculty at Duke. He is a widower with two young daughters, Emilee, 10, and Amelia, 8. (Their mother was French.) They are delightful girls and so much fun. I've fallen in love with them. I've also fallen in love with their father, Dr. Michael Carlson. He is a fine man, and I know you two will get along very well.

With your blessing, we would like to be married at The Retreat in April. We're planning a small ceremony — just Michael and me and the girls, but of course we want you and Bob to stand up with us.

Please write back as soon as you can to let me know if this is OK. I hope this is not too much of a shock!

I can't thank you enough for everything you have done for me, especially the night you saved me and Bob. You will forever have a piece of my heart.

Always,
Hazel

Bill read the letter three times, sitting out on the porch, sipping whiskey.

He was happy for Hazel. He knew they wouldn't end up together. Still, it stung, he could admit that to himself. But he'd never tell her. He wrote back immediately saying he'd be thrilled to host a wedding at The Retreat — a first. He encouraged her to write Kent to let him know what they'd need.

Bill knew enough to understand that when a woman said she wanted a small wedding it didn't mean she wanted a simple wedding.

Fortunately, Kent's wife Katie would know exactly what needed to be done. After he dropped the letter into outgoing mail, he called her to let her know there would be a wedding soon. Katie adored Hazel and said she would be more than happy to help. She was so excited, especially being the mother of four sons.

A lovely wedding

The Retreat was the scene of a lovely wedding the afternoon of April 14, 1962.

Hazel had planned to wear her best Sunday dress, but her husband-to-be would hear nothing of it. Michael gave her his gold American Express card — a new-fangled thing at the time — and sent her to Charlotte to buy whatever her heart desired.

She had already started looking before she left for the big-city outing. Hazel fell in love with a pink ball gown that had graced the cover of Modern Bride the previous December. It had accents of French lace and was divine.

The ladies at Montaldo's insisted she buy it. The groom would be knocked off his feet, they assured her. She used a credit card for the first time in her life. She felt like a queen. The ladies even sent her home with dyed pink shoes to match — and an enviable trousseau, especially all the delicate lingerie.

Next, Hazel designed dresses for her soon-to-be daughters. Emilee and Amelia's French grand-mére had shipped yards of Alençon lace from Paris. Katie offered to sew the flower girl dresses for her. She had always made play clothes for her boys, but this was a new challenge which she accepted with zest and determination. Katie had won many 4-H ribbons for sewing in school. She also won special recognition for a community cookbook. Kent and Katie met at a state 4-H competition when he was showing his family's prized beef cattle, and she was racking up even more sewing ribbons.

Katie wanted to create dresses for Emilee and Amelia that were finely detailed and ethereal. She took Grand-mére's lace and sat down with Hazel to create the design. The tea-length dresses were perfect, and the girls squealed with delight when they saw them. They looked like princesses when they put the dresses on.

Bill insisted on buying flowers for the wedding. He'd known Hazel for so long, and he knew that tulips were her favorite flower. It cost him a mint, but he picked out a delicate bouquet of white tulips tied with a white satin bow. For the girls, the florist made wreaths of pink miniature rosebuds, baby's breath, and pale pink ribbons for their hair.

He snuck a swatch of Hazel's wedding gown after it had been altered and took it to the florist to ensure the roses matched perfectly. They felt grown up as they walked through the front yard to their father, who was standing at the front steps of The Lodge. Bill then escorted Hazel, with Bob walking behind them. It was a short, sweet service with the pastor of Bill and Bob's church presiding.

Bill pulled out all the stops for the wedding supper, held out on the wraparound porch. The spring evening was perfect. He served steaks from his own herd, grilled to order, twice-baked potatoes, salad, Katie's famous sourdough rolls, and, as a surprise, hand-churned peach ice cream from peaches that Katie had frozen the summer before. The good thing about having four sons was that they were always eager churners to get a creamy bowl of ice cream in reward. It couldn't have been a more perfect evening.

Bill brought out expensive champagne to toast the happy couple. The girls were thoroughly fascinated by Grandfather Hugh, and stayed glued to his side the whole day. He thought they were simply adorable. He let them take tiny tastes of his champagne when they thought nobody was looking.

Sitting around the table with family and friends, Bill was happy that he'd pulled off such a special day for Hazel. He couldn't help but feel a little smug that she had belonged to him before Michael. He'd never share that with Michael. Being a psychiatrist, the other man had probably already figured it out. Across the table, Bob was having the same smug thoughts.

Hazel and Michael honeymooned in Paris — the girls flew with them and stayed with Grand-pére and Grand-mére LaPierre, who fell in love with Hazel just as their granddaughters had. Hazel learned some basic French so she could greet the LaPierres properly.

After a month, the family returned to the States and settled in their new home. Michael had insisted on building a new, larger home for Hazel. The girls now had their own bedrooms. They thought that was the best thing ever. When the girls returned to school in the fall, so did Hazel.

She started studying for her master's degree — which her new husband paid for — to become a counselor to help abused women. She took a couple of courses a semester so that she could be involved in the girls' lives, shuttling them to piano, violin, French lessons, and ballet lessons. Michael and Hazel believed in keeping them active. They agreed that they should embrace and appreciate their French heritage.

After completing her degree, Hazel became a trailblazer in her new field.

Bill and Bob attended her graduation ceremony and were so proud of her. Each year, they got a Christmas card from Hazel and her family. They were happy that she was so happy. She deserved it. She had had enough tragedy in her life already.

Bob wasn't surprised when his father sold the brokerage office on January 1, 1962, the year Bob graduated from undergrad. It had been a good run, but mills were starting to set up their own purchasing departments. Bill's health wasn't great, and fortuitously, he met an interested buyer. He was approached by a mill owner in Gaston County and got an excellent price. He helped them set up their purchasing department, insuring a successful transition. Betty stayed on with Bill, managing accounts for The Retreat and taking care of his investments. She worked for him until she retired.

That spring, Hugh was diagnosed with lung cancer. He'd rolled his own cigarettes for years. It finally caught up with him. He moved into The Lodge with Bill, spending his last months reading, resting, and occasionally walking with the hunting dogs when he felt like it. Hugh brought with him the bed he'd shared with his beloved wife, his chest of drawers, and his bedside table. Bill also took Hugh up in his Piper Cub for short jaunts. He loved seeing the property from the air.

A painful departure

In May 1962, Bob was set to graduate from Duke. He was headed to med school a couple of months later. He should have been on top of the world, but he wasn't.

Bob had been seeing Barb Flowers for a year or so. She was a neat gal. He'd met her when he was at Woodberry, and she was at Chatham. She was from a good family in Virginia. She loved The Retreat. She loved Hugh and she adored Bill.

Barb's parents did not get along, so she treasured the time she and Bob had. It got her away from her parents. Like most women of that era, Barb was ready to get married and have children. Bob wasn't ready, and didn't know how to tell her that. He decided to hold off as long as he could. He didn't want to ruin what would be their last night together.

The night before Bob was set to graduate, he had his cap and gown in the closet, ready to go. Barb brought a black dress and heels and her overnight bag to his little apartment at The Retreat. Bill had gone to South America for an annual commodity traders' meeting. He hated to miss graduation, he told Bob, but he was the association's president, so he didn't have a choice.

"Dad, it's no big deal," Bob assured him. "Go and have a good time."

Barb and Bob invited a few friends over and grilled hamburgers. They listened to the stereo on full blast, danced, and drank beer until they exhausted themselves around 2 that morning. Barb and Bob crashed. They snuggled next to each another and went to sleep as Bob's tropical fish looked on from their aquarium.

Bob woke up a few hours later. It was raining. He raised the window and felt the rain. The cool, cool rain.

“What the hell am I going to do,” he asked himself.

Bob looked at Barb, fast asleep in his bed. She looked like an angel. He looked back into the closet at her black dress and his cap and gown.

“To hell with it,” he said, and crawled back in bed with Barb.

Bob couldn’t face it after all. He felt like a coward when he ended up writing Barb a letter before starting at Duke’s Med School, explaining how he felt. He never heard from her, but when he went home for Christmas, Bob learned from his father that she was engaged to one of Bob’s classmates from Woodberry. It was a good match. He didn’t blame her, and he wasn’t bitter.

He hoped she wasn’t, either.

Another large dose of pain

Hugh Davis Henderson died Aug. 4, 1962, the same day the world mourned Marilyn Monroe's passing. As much as Bob adored that movie star, he loved his grandfather much more and would miss him terribly over the years. He was a giant in Bob's life, his North Star. His funeral was in the college chapel in their small town. The place was packed. It was like a reunion for Hugh's friends. Many of Bill's and Bob's friends came to support them.

With the money Bob inherited from his grandfather, he was able to go to medical school debt-free. This was unheard of in the 1960s — or any time a student goes to medical school.

Bill wanted his son to go to the best medical school. Since money was not an issue and Bob's grades were impeccable, he was accepted into medical school at Duke. He got a fair amount of ribbing from his Woodberry Forest buddies, most of whom had gone to Carolina. They'd stayed on in Chapel Hill for business school or pharmacy school. Bob didn't care. Duke was the best, as far as he and his father were concerned. Bob wanted to make his father proud and honor his grandfather's memory.

As another generous gift, Bill bought Bob a dark blue Corvette and sent him off to Durham. Bob didn't get a single ticket the entire time he had that car. Not that he didn't enjoy the speed of the low-slung sportscar, he was just careful where he did it. And he resisted most peer pressure to go full throttle around Durham and surrounding counties, like Orange. Person County had some lonely country roads, but Bob didn't want any trouble.

He did well in medical school, making excellent grades. Bob was proud of himself, and Bill was, too. After graduation, Bill told Bob to take a year off and travel around Europe.

Bob couldn't turn down that offer.

Traveling alone and outgoing by nature and necessity, he met some interesting people. There were many other people his age traveling then. Eurail passes were dirt cheap, and hostels were clean and safe. Nobody minded bunking together. Wherever Bob went, he ended up sharing a meal with young people who had mind-blowing ideas. After all, it was the 1960s, the Age of Aquarius. Experimentation of all kinds ran rampant. He didn't overindulge. In medical school, he learned how drugs and alcohol affected the human body — one too many autopsies proved that. And he'd seen what his father went through with the morphine.

He was curious about his peers, and what their thoughts were concerning life with a capital "L."

They scarfed down flaky croissants in Paris, sampled strong coffee in Istanbul, sipped fabulous wine and ate endless plates of pasta in Tuscany. Bob indulged his appetites without overindulging. He patted himself on the back, figuring he did a pretty good job for a single man without a care in the world.

He'd learned a lot from his mother's tragedy and Buck's drunken rages, too. Addiction was a real problem in his family, so he was very wary. He figured eating good food was the least of the possible vices.

Bob eventually fell in with a group of guys all headed for graduate schools of one kind or another. They had a lot in common and got along well, making easy travel companions.

In Spain, they settled down to a tapas dinner in Madrid. A few of the guys would be starting coursework in January, just a few weeks away. It was a farewell dinner for the merry band of travelers.

It was a night full of conversation in the late hours where you share your deepest fears with those you have grown to trust. They'd had a ton of fun, but could grow serious, too. The sangria flowed freely.

Bob was telling the guys that with med school behind him, it was time to select a specialty. He'd enjoyed all his rotations and was in a conundrum. His father had always encouraged him to specialize, because he knew Bob would make more money than family doctors or internists. Bill had a knack for making money, just like his father, Hugh.

What to do?

"Man, Bob, I sure wish you'd help me with Little John," Big John said, and they all laughed. Big John was indeed a big guy, beefy and tall, and Little John was the name he'd given his privates. They all got a kick out of that the night he'd told them in Paris. None of the others had such a nickname — at least that they'd admit to the group.

"What's the problem?" Bob asked him.

He looked sheepish. You'd think because of his size that Big John would have trouble getting women, but he was charming and hilarious. There was no woman he couldn't charm. They'd all witnessed that as they'd traveled the continent together. You make a woman laugh, he'd tell us, and you're halfway home — maybe more so.

Bob was shocked at what he said next.

"Well, you know, Bob, I like my sangria," he said, gesturing to the pitchers on the table. "And I like all the wine, and I like beer."

Everyone knew that.

"The problem is, Little John doesn't like it so much, and dang it, I don't like that!"

That was another thing about Big John. He never used profanity. His creativity with what he called bad words was admirable.

"And sometimes, you know, with all the travel and all the late nights, I'm just tired, and well, so is Little John," he finished, looking dejected. "You know I can't let the ladies down."

"I know you can't, John," Bob said, and everyone in the group nodded empathetically. Whether or not they wanted to admit it, it had happened to all of them at one time or another. Yeah, it was mostly after drinking too much. They recognized that. But they also knew from eavesdropping around their fathers and grandfathers and uncles that the problem would only get worse as the years added up.

"Hey, Bob!" said Jimmy, who would soon return to Chapel Hill for an MBA, "Why don't you study urology? Figure out a way to make all the Little Johns of the world stand at attention!"

The rest of the guys laughed. Bob didn't. He had that entrepreneurial mind that ran in the Henderson family.

"You know, Jimmy, that's not a bad idea," he said. "Not bad at all."

That January, while still traveling, Bob applied to Johns Hopkins. He was accepted in May and began a three-year urology residency that July. He was on his way.

Urology was fascinating, and he thought he could make a difference. He wanted to open a urology practice when he graduated and start a lab simultaneously.

He wrote to his father, asking him to loan him the money needed, and Bill wrote back immediately to say yes. Bob was going to get to the bottom of Big John's problem. Bill didn't say anything about it, but he'd been having the same problem. High blood pressure ran in the Henderson family, and his medicine was making him feel lousy.

Bob graduated in May 1969, and again, Bill encouraged him to wait a few months before beginning work. The residency had been grueling, although rewarding. Bob was grateful for a break.

Source of inspiration

That May, Bob rented a small apartment, telling his father he wanted to live in town for a while, get a feel for the place, decide where to practice. He wanted to meet people his own age, maybe even think about settling down. He was, he thought to himself, going to turn 30 the next year. That was nearly "confirmed bachelor" status. Bob wanted to find the right woman.

He found a comfortable one-room apartment over the grocery store downtown. It was inexpensive and clean. Myrtle Jackson, who owned the store with her husband, Fred, was always giving him outdated cans of food — "They're fine, dear, we just can't sell them anymore," she'd say — as well as slightly damaged fruits that were also fine to eat. "You know how picky these housewives are."

Mr. Jackson would slip Bob a T-bone every now and again from the butcher counter, where he held court six days a week, or maybe some ground beef which was about to expire — so he said — Bob knew it was fine.

"We can't have our young doctor going hungry, now, can we?" he'd say.

They pretty much adopted Bob as their own son. They'd never had children. Bob was fine with the arrangement because really, what young adult turns down free food? The Jacksons had graciously put a hot plate and refrigerator upstairs, so he was happy as a clam, and well-fed, to boot.

Bob did his part, too, lugging an extra mattress from The Retreat, his mother's card table and the matching chairs she'd left behind, and his grandfather's favorite easy chair. He threw in a couple of bean bag chairs from Thompson's Furniture right next door, a few mismatched lamps from The Retreat, and he was set.

The Jacksons said sleeping on the floor simply would not do. They bought a bed frame from Thompson's. It was not a problem, they said. They got a professional discount. They even got free delivery one door down. It made Bob chuckle when Mrs. Jackson told him.

"We'll simply keep it for our next renter."

The term "renter" had a pretty loose definition for the Jacksons. They barely let Bob pay them anything.

"You have to save your money to get your practice established soon," Mr. Jackson said. "And it will be so nice to have a doctor in the family."

He looked at Bob sheepishly.

"You're absolutely right, Mr. Jackson. You and Mrs. Jackson can come see me any time. No appointment necessary."

"Hey, Myrtle! Did you hear that?" Mr. Jackson yelled to the front of the store. "We are going to be Robert's first patients!" The Jacksons were the only friends who ever called Bob by his given name. It was endearing.

"Yes, dear, I heard," said Mrs. Jackson from her usual spot at the cash register, not missing a beat as she rang up Mrs. Weaver's order.

It wasn't long before Bob started having company at his bachelor pad. There was a set of steps at the back of the building, which he used to enter and exit, as did his visitors. The entrance was discreet and private, and he was glad. The most memorable friends were two college-age girls who were home for the summer. They told him they were best friends and did everything together. It wasn't long before they found out Bob had his own apartment and started coming over.

"That's so groovy!" they said in unison.

They said a lot of things in unison, and often finished one another's sentences. They didn't seem to mind the age difference.

"Ohmigosh Bobby, you're way more mature than the boys we go to college with," Girl One said.

"Like, waaaaaay more," Girl Two echoed.

Bobby? That was a first. Bob went with it.

The trio ended up hanging out together a lot of evenings. It was a fun, carefree time. They laughed a lot. Bob laughed more than he had in a long time, maybe ever. Sure, he had fun with the guys in Europe, but this was different.

"Waaaaaay different," as Girl Two was fond of saying.

One evening in early August, they came over for their final visit before leaving for school.

It was nearly the anniversary of Marilyn Monroe's death. She'd died just seven years earlier. The girls were obsessed with her. Ouija boards were in their heyday. Girl One had just gotten one for her birthday in July, and they were absolutely convinced they could raise Marilyn using the Ouija board.

Like his grandfather, Bob had gotten into the habit of having an evening whiskey. That evening, before the girls arrived, He had two drinks. Why not? Summer was ending and it seemed a fine time for a celebration, to wish the girls well before they left for the fall semester. He also needed to get serious about hanging his shingle.

"Before we get out the Ouija board, we've got to cleanse ourselves," he told the girls.

They were all for it. In a matter of seconds, they stripped off their halter tops, cutoffs, and panties. They all took a shower together, which was a hoot considering how small the bathroom was. Bob made a mental note to put in a large shower when he built his own home. Then they wrapped themselves in towels and sat cross-legged on the floor. Girl Two shut off all the lights. The only light was from Bob's two aquariums.

Girl One decided to light a few candles to further set the mood. Candles and incense were all the rage back then. Bob had Steppenwolf playing low on the stereo. The girls leaned over and kissed each other — a big kiss. Then, one by one, they kissed Bob. They passed a joint back and forth and Bob nursed his whiskey. Their towels slipped. They didn't care. Ah, youth.

They tried to raise Marilyn. The Ouija board was not forthcoming, but something else rose. That new bed ended up coming in handy that night, although as soon as he could afford it, Bob bought a larger mattress.

After the girls left in the wee hours of the morning, He drank some ice water before going to bed. He needed the hydration.

"Boy, if I could somehow bottle those girls' lack of inhibition, I could be rich one day. Wildly rich," he chuckled to himself.

Then he remembered what John had said that night in Madrid.

Bob knew what he wanted to do with his life.

When everything fell apart

Because Bob wanted to be near his father, he accepted a coveted position with an established urology practice in his hometown in the fall of 1971. Although he'd had a charmed life through college, med school and residency, working in a practice was totally different. The other doctors checked on him frequently, asked him to explain his treatment choices. They emphasized patient care and talked about community relations.

"You might be brilliant, Bob, but you have to be a good doctor, too," the founding partner told him.

The patients quickly shortened "Dr. Robert" to "Dr. Bob." That suited him well.

Over the years, as doctors retired or moved, he became a senior partner and helped to hire a knowledgeable group.

The five of them got along well, and Bob was pleased. Their areas of interest did not overlap. He still had the idea of developing a drug to improve libido, but that had to go on the back burner as he refined the practice. Then he got married — unfortunately.

He couldn't see it at first, but Bob's wife Jennifer ended up being just like his mother. She was interested in nothing more than playing bridge at the club, sitting by the pool, and spending money. Good Lord, could that woman spend money.

That should have been a red flag, but he was so busy with the practice and with trying to keep her happy that he honestly didn't notice. He wanted to start a family right away, but Jenny told him a year later that she wasn't interested in having children. They didn't talk about it before they got married. They only dated for a few months. Bob just assumed she would want to have his babies. It hurt, but he had to let that dream go. She wasn't budging.

That should have been another red flag. It was his father's disastrous choice in women all over again. Bob was not the golden boy he thought he would be. Success was one thing, but his personal life was looking like a failure.

Meanwhile, the practice's longtime business manager retired, and Jenny immediately began lobbying Bob to hire her brother Paul.

Paul Pulliam had an impeccable resumé, Bob had to admit. He was a CPA and had a law degree from the University of North Carolina at Chapel Hill. He seemed the right fit for the practice and Bob hoped it would smooth things with Jenny. With the blessing of his partners, Bob hired him.

Huge mistake.

For the first few years, everything seemed perfect. The practice was thriving and successful. Bob was happy, and he thought Jenny was, too, finally.

Then came the day he was called into the conference room with the other four partners. He thought they were meeting with a drug rep. Instead, he found the police chief sitting at the head of the table. He'd known Steve Chambers all his life. Everybody in McNeill County knew everybody else. Steve graduated from McNeill County High School and received his associate degree in criminal justice from McNeill County Community College. He'd been with the police department ever since. He'd been chief for the past 10 years. He was known as a hard worker and was well respected in the small community.

"Steve, great to see you," Bob said, extending his hand. He

did not reciprocate. He wore a serious expression.

"Dr. Henderson, please sit down. I wish I were here under better circumstances, but this is a formal call."

Bob sat down in his usual seat, confused. The chief had always called him Bob. That's when he noticed his partners were sitting with their heads bowed, as if in prayer.

"Steve, what exactly is going on?"

"Dr. Henderson don't take me for a fool. At least treat me with the respect my position deserves."

Bob took a deep breath and tried to keep calm.

"Steve," Bob said, his voice even, "I swear I don't know why you're here."

"Okay, Dr. Henderson, if that's the way you want to play this. You've been under investigation for the past three months."

"WHAT?" Bob cried, leaping to his feet.

"Sit down, Dr. Henderson," Steve said, his face now a hardened mask. Bob had no idea what was going on, but he tried to calm himself. Again, nobody met his gaze.

Whatever this was, it was not good.

Then he remembered a meeting of the partners three months ago. The practice had been making money hand over fist. They all had as many patients as they could comfortably handle, but something wasn't making sense. The draws were not what they should be.

The partners unanimously voted to hire an independent

forensic CPA firm to conduct a wide-sweeping investigation. Bob recused himself, although he agreed with the partners that they should not alert Paul. Instead, the firm came in to gather evidence during Paul's three-week European vacation. They'd promised they'd be in touch as soon as they had something.

That day had come.

It was then Bob noticed Paul was in the room, too, seated in the corner.

"Okay, Chief Chambers, what do you have to say to me?"

Before he could answer, Paul stood and spoke up.

"Bob, I'm so sorry. I had no idea you had been stealing from the practice. The other partners know it, too. I'm sorry it's come to this. If you and Jenny needed money, you should have asked. You know I would have helped. I consider you a brother."

His voice dripped with mock sincerity. Bob's face went white, and he felt, for a second, that he might pass out, then he flushed hot as fire and began to feel sick to his stomach. He didn't know whether to sit still or punch Paul in the face. He was having a hard time realizing his partners were against him, too.

He sat.

He thought to himself, "That lying SOB! The day I hired him, I knew I'd regret it one day. I was right. I knew Jenny was involved. The cars, the clothes, the furs, the trips. Whatever money Paul had stolen from me had been funneled to Jenny as well.

"Dammit."
Bob could barely focus on what Chief Chambers was saying.

The investigation found that nearly $10 million could not be accounted for over a 10-year period. The other partners finally confronted Bob, silently making eye contact.

He was completely blindsided.

Paul told the chief, "I suspected something hasn't been right. I hate to blame Bob, but that's the only place I can see where the money has been diverted."

Set up.

Bob couldn't think straight. For years, he later discovered, Paul had forged checks with Bob's name on them that couldn't be traced to the missing money.
He felt a cold knife plunge into his heart.

"Can't you see I'm being set up?" he pleaded with his partners.

No one said a word.

Bob found out later that his "secret account" was accessed by his snake of a brother-in-law. The money was gone, nowhere to be found.

"My God!" Bob whispered.

He said nothing as Chief Chambers asked him to leave with him. He did Bob the courtesy of not cuffing him, but it still hurt. He vowed to get even with Paul, and Jenny, too.

"That bitch."

After Bob got home from processing at the police station, he found a goodbye letter and a divorce petition on the kitchen table. "Damn, she did work fast."

He thought about calling his father Bill, but there was really nothing he could do. He'd started having some minor heart problems, and Bob definitely didn't want to burden him with this.

He had no one to turn to. His so-called friends had believed every lie. That's what stung. No one had questioned Paul or the charges.

Bob called Brad Jacobs, his attorney, along with Eugene Smith, his CPA. They knew Paul by reputation, and they wouldn't put it past him, they each told Bob. Thus far, he hadn't gotten caught. They did believe Bob, but they couldn't really help him. Bob thought Paul was family and would do the right thing when it came to the practice.

He was dead wrong.

Eugene told Bob, "Your brother-in-law has done this in such a slick and elaborate way, we can't prove you didn't take the money."

"Dammit."

The divorce went through. Jenny got the house in the country club. Bob moved back to The Retreat before the trial was to begin, telling his father as little as he could. Bill didn't really care about the details — he was glad to have his son home. He'd never liked Jenny but kept quiet. Bob wished he could reach out to his father's old buddies, but they were either dead or moved on. Bill had gotten an excellent deal from the convenience store sales and continued to oversee his investments, as well as managing the property with

Kent's help.

Bob's trial was over quickly, an open-and-shut case. On the bright side, he was only sentenced to five years in prison, the lowest possible sentence. Although it was a lot of money, he had a clean record. On the not-so-bright side, he lost the medical license he'd worked so hard to get. Brad would file an appeal, and told Bob that he could apply for reinstatement once he'd served his time. He would have to wait five years. Bob would re-apply as soon as he was released.

Judge Victor Adams called him into chambers after the sentencing.

"Son, I hate the way things came out for you. I know you didn't do this. I've known your father for years and I admired your grandfather a great deal. You were not raised to do something like this."

"Thank you, Judge Adams. I appreciate your saying that."

He raised his palm.

"Be that as it may, I knew there was no reason to recuse myself. This case was not winnable. It stunk to high heaven. And I know it's because of Paul Pulliam. I wish there were something I could have done to help. Your appeal will take some time, I'm afraid."

"Thank you, Judge."

"Listen, son. Be smart, keep your head down, do your time, and come home safe. I have known Warden Solomon Dixon for years. He's a good man. He'll give you a fair shake."

"Yes, sir. I'll take your advice. I have no desire to stir up any kind of trouble for myself."

"See that you don't." The judge rose and shook Bob's hand, then nodded to the bailiff by the door who was quietly waiting to escort Bob to prison.

He took a deep breath and walked out of the judge's office.

Intake day

The bailiff led Bob out to a waiting prison van. He was the last inmate to board. There were 11 others in the van, all sitting quietly, all handcuffed. He had no idea why they were there, and didn't want to know. He took his place on the end of the first row of seats. The bailiff slid the door shut and locked it.

They say the smell of fear is only a literary device. That day Bob wasn't so sure. He could tell some of the inmates were sweating profusely, despite the air conditioning blasting on them. Others sat stone faced. This wasn't their first rodeo; they knew what to expect. Bob had no clue.

The van drove through town, and in a few minutes, they reached the looming Piedmont Correctional Institution. If they'd designed the 11-story brick building to look imposing, it worked.

They were led into a reception area through a series of locked doors, each making a horrible scraping sound as it slammed shut. A corrections officer reviewed Bob's papers to make sure everything was in order. He was taken to a small holding room that was empty save for a bench bolted to the wall. He knew what was coming next. The corrections officer asked him to remove his clothes. Knowing he wouldn't get his clothing back, he'd changed before he left the courthouse into a plain white undershirt, an old pair of khakis, and an old pair of loafers. No belt. The officer then performed a thorough search. Bob knew he was just doing his job and complied with whatever he asked. He tried to imagine it was a regular physical — just more invasive than normal.

The officer had a T-shirt, overshirt, a pair of underwear, pants, socks, and shoes. He told Bob to dress and left the room, closing and locking the door. Bob dressed quickly, then rapped gently on the door. The guard led him to a table in the intake area, where he received an identical set of clothes along with bedding and a toiletry kit.

Next, Bob went to a nurse who drew blood and did a quick health screening. Later in the week, he had a more thorough physical, a mental health screening, and a dental check. He was particular about his teeth and had seen a dentist every six months his whole life. He was relieved to find there was a dental clinic on-site. Then he went for educational testing. He filled out the MMPI, a psychological form he was familiar with from med school.

After the initial intake, Bob was led to his cell, a single room with a twin bed. The door had a narrow vertical window. The bed had a pillow at the head of the bed, with two plain sheets, a pillowcase, and a blanket neatly folded at the foot. He quickly made the bed, deciding to lie down just a few minutes to rest his eyes. Thanks to his years of medical training, he could fall asleep anywhere, and fast.

The next thing he knew, he heard the announcement for

supper, got up, splashed some water on his face, washed his hands, and left the cell.

Bob wasn't expecting much from the food, but it wasn't bad. He knew the prison system had to provide inmates with a certain number of calories each day, on what he assumed was a limited budget. In a population like this, you had to make sure the inmates were well fed and treated with a measure of respect.

One of the officers had told Bob as much earlier in the afternoon: "We'll treat you good and feed you as good as we can. We will give you something to do and allow you recreation and visitation. We don't expect to have a problem with you, Mr. Henderson."

He didn't correct him by saying Dr. Henderson. Within these walls, Bob was no longer a doctor.

"No, sir, you will not," Bob assured him.

Bob's stay at Piedmont was brief since it was an intake center for the western part of the state. Within the week, he was sent to Raleigh.

Meeting the warden

Solomon Dixon, the warden of Central Prison in Raleigh, was a solid, Christian man who tried to treat every prisoner with dignity — from the white-collar embezzler to the hardened serial killer. They just had to be respectful and obedient.

When Bob sat down with Dixon, he explained exactly what happened to him. He was sure the warden would take his side.

"I know every prisoner you meet tells you this, but I am innocent of the crime for which I was convicted. Let me tell you my story."

Dixon listened without interrupting. "You tell a convincing story. I just need to check it out," Dixon said. "I have some contacts in McNeill County."

The warden had seen it before – a man so wrapped up in his work that he didn't pay much attention to the details of the business. Men like that hired people to take care of finances. And some of those people were clever as hell and knew how to take exactly what they wanted and point the finger at the clueless victim.

The warden knew Bob could not practice medicine or even assist in the infirmary. Instead, Bob asked to work as a janitor around the infirmary and small hospital in the prison. That was as close as he would be allowed to get. He understood. The warden said that would be fine. He was pleased to have a cooperative inmate. After all, his crime involved no violence.

What piqued Dixon's interest, however, is what Bob said after he thanked the warden for the job.

"I'm a urologist by training, and I'm working on a formula

that would improve the sex lives of both men and women, as far as desire is concerned. I'm hoping to continue my research while I'm here. My father has always encouraged me to be goal oriented. Here, my goals are to stay positive, make the best use of my time, and remain a contributing member of society."

That impressed the warden. He could tell that Bob was intelligent and polite. He'd been raised right. He was, though, too sure of himself.

"That seems to be a reasonable request. I'm sorry I can't let you work in the labs here, but it's prison regulations. I'm sure you understand. What I can do is house you in the hospital wing to give you a private room, and it's right next to the library. You're welcome to use the library whenever you finish your janitorial work. If you'd like more books, you can have your father mail new books to you. Regulations state that they'll be thoroughly examined before they are checked into the library. If you could leave them with us once your time comes to an end, I'd be most grateful."

"Sure thing, Warden Dixon. I'd also be happy to tutor any of my colleagues for their GED and ESL classes. I'm fluent in Spanish from the time my father and I spent in Argentina."

"I'll consider that. I hope it will make your time with us fruitful and that it will pass quickly. Let me call the hospital wing, and I'll have you escorted back to your cell so you can get your things."

In the back of his mind, Warden Dixon wondered if Bob was just a slick conman, but he was willing to give him a chance while he checked out the details of his conviction.

The two men shook hands, and Bob left the warden's office. It didn't take him long to grab what was in his cell: two more prison-issued uniforms, two sets of underwear, a pair of flip flops, his toiletries, his Bible, the latest copy of the Physicians' Desk Reference, and his well-used and well-loved college anatomy book — the three books he couldn't bear to leave behind. His father had sent them to the prison and the books had been examined and approved.

After the door closed, Dixon leaned back in his chair, fingers steepled together, lost in thought.

He and his wife had tried to have children for years. When Marie finally went in for bloodwork, her doctor discovered she had early-stage ovarian cancer. She had to have a complete hysterectomy, which killed her sex drive. Dixon wasn't the kind of man to push things, but wouldn't it be wonderful to have that part of their marriage back?

He was cautious about Bob, but Judge Adams had told him the Hendersons were a good family, one that had worked hard and found success. Adams said it was unlikely that Bob was an embezzler. The Hendersons had plenty of money. Dixon decided to give Bob what he could within the confines of his role — and to be among the first volunteers when it was time to test the drug. As crazy as it seemed, he wanted to trust this inmate. This had never happened before. Maybe everyone behind bars wasn't guilty after all.

"Sure," the warden thought to himself, "I must be getting soft." But thinking of Marie always made him smile, and when his secretary came in to bring the mail, he had a huge grin on his face.

She didn't ask the warden about it but wondered what was going on. Solomon Dixon rarely smiled at work.

A woman named Mindy Tanner had been processed into Women's Prison in Raleigh the same day that Bob entered the penal system. Their lives would not cross until years later.

After her intake, Mindy had a similar conversation with her warden.

Warden John Jeffries at Women's Prison and Dixon were old friends. They liked to talk about interesting inmates. Jeffries had just met Mindy Tanner, convicted, she said, falsely, of tax evasion. The wardens talked about the coincidence – Bob's financial crime, and Mindy's. Dixon joked they must have had the same accountant.

Dixon made a note to tell Bob about Mindy once he was released. Jeffries thought the two might end up meeting during post-incarceration rehabilitation. Recently released prisoners needed every friend they could get on the outside.

Mindy

Mindy Jordan was a native of Marietta, Ga. She grew up on a farm and loved animals. She rode horses and nurtured a number of cats and dogs. She tried to name the chickens until her mother explained to 6-year-old Mindy where their Sunday dinners came from. Mindy thought about becoming a vegetarian, but decided she couldn't give up her mommy's fried chicken.

Everybody loved Mindy. She was a good girl and made excellent grades. She wanted to be a veterinarian until she joined the Future Health Professionals Club in high school. That set her on a path to nursing.

Mindy dated clean-cut guys. Her steady in high school was the quarterback and she was the head cheerleader. Everybody assumed they would marry — until homecoming night senior year, when she caught him behind the bleachers with one of her best friends.

Mindy dried her tears and headed to Emory University,

graduating in three years with a nursing degree in May 1980. She took a job at Grady Memorial as an emergency room nurse.

She met Abner "Bulldog" Tanner there a month later. He worked with his father in a small construction business, and had cut his hand pretty badly as he was showing a piece of equipment to a newly hired sub.

At least that's what he told Mindy. He'd actually left work early — it was a Friday, after all — and headed to the Sassy Saucer, his local strip club-watering hole. A few beers in, he got into a scuffle with said sub, who slashed his hand with a broken beer bottle.

After the ER doc stitched Bulldog up, the patient promptly asked Mindy for her number. For all his rough edges, he was handsome and had a certain swagger about him. Even though he was a bad boy, he could turn on the charm, and that appealed to Mindy.

Why not take a chance?

Bulldog came from a broken home. Both he and Mindy had worked part-time jobs in high school to make money. Mindy didn't need to work, but her parents, Quentin and Katherine, instilled a strong work ethic in her from an early age. Mindy's money went into a savings account for incidentals she'd need during nursing school. Her parents footed her school tuition, but she wanted to buy her own townhouse as soon as she graduated. Bulldog worked for his dad's company even though he didn't care about it. He only wanted money for gas and beer. His lack of ambition was astonishing.

A week after they met, Bulldog took Mindy to a nice restaurant in Atlanta — on his daddy's company credit card — and started pouring on the charm.

Even though Mindy had dated in high school, she'd never been intimate with a man. She wasn't a prude, but it wasn't the way she was raised. Her parents held high expectations for her and Mandy, her twin sister. Mandy worked downtown at one of the city's top architectural firms.

Once Mindy started dating Bulldog, she realized he was very different from her quarterback boyfriend in high school. He was a rough and tumble man, and she was a naïve woman. She was filled with desire for him because he was so different, and she told him so.

"But I was raised a certain way, and it's hard to change."

"Don't worry about it, baby. There's no rush."

He was older and more experienced. He had to be, she reasoned. She was touched by his gentleness.

It made her want him all the more.

After several dates, they went to his uncle's place at the river one Sunday afternoon. They cruised around in the pontoon boat, dropping anchor to sunbathe for several hours. Bulldog had a cooler full of beer for himself and chilled Chardonnay for Mindy. It was a lazy afternoon. Mindy was off the next day, so she didn't have to worry about how much she drank.

Alcohol had an immediate effect on Mindy, stripping her of her inhibitions and magnifying her desire. She was becoming frustrated.

That night at the cabin, Mindy drank the last of the bottle of wine while Bulldog sipped beer and watched television. Nothing was on — just summer re-runs.

Mindy excused herself from the den.

A few minutes later, she came back dressed in a black bikini bottom with a condom in the side. Bulldog was pleasantly surprised. He cut off the TV, and Mindy danced seductively for him.

Bulldog soon took her hands in his.

"I want you so much," Mindy said.

"I know you do, baby, but I want your first time to be special. Not in some old, dusty lake cabin."

"I can't wait much longer."

"Why don't we get married?"

"What?"

That got Mindy's attention.

"Why not? We love each other. We both have good jobs. We can have a good life together."

"We love each other?"

"Yes, baby. I love you."

"I love you, too," Mindy said, realizing she did. At least in that moment, with the help of the wine.

The next morning, they drove to the Fulton County Probate Court. They were first in line when the doors opened at 8:30 a.m. Bulldog paid for their marriage license, then they went up to the second floor. Mindy wore a yellow sundress with white flip-flops and Bulldog had a polo shirt and shorts. They didn't care. On the way, Bulldog had stopped in a field near the lake and cut a single sunflower for Mindy — her favorite flower.

The ceremony took just minutes.

They drove straight to Mindy's townhouse and consummated their marriage in her queen-sized bed, one of her first purchases when she went to work for the hospital.

They stayed in bed the rest of the day. Bulldog got up early in the afternoon to bring Mindy a bowl of cereal. She still ate Lucky Charms. He didn't tease her because that was his childhood favorite, too.

Mindy was glad she waited until her wedding day, but now she knew why some of her high school girlfriends had made such a big deal about sex. It was indeed a big deal — and Bulldog knew what he was doing.

He had been living in one of the construction office's trailers, so he only had his clothes and few incidentals to bring to Mindy's two-bedroom townhouse. She'd never had a roommate, but Mindy's parents had insisted she buy a two-bedroom because of the resale value. Truth be told, Quentin and Katherine bought the townhouse for her. She was paying them back to earn equity.

She thought about mentioning this to Bulldog, but something in the back of her mind said maybe she should just keep it to herself.

The Mob comes to Atlanta

Ever since he had seen "The Godfather" as a kid, Bulldog had been fascinated by the idea of being a member of the Mafia. They could do whatever they wanted, and people were afraid of them.

But he also knew the Mafia didn't exist in the South, not that he knew of. One day, he met Joey, a sub who had moved to Atlanta from New York City. The guy's family was originally from Italy — Sicily, to be exact. He was a proud second-generation Italian American. Bulldog began peppering him with questions about the Mob. Did he know anyone in it? Had anyone in his family ever been in it? He confessed he had always wanted to be a part of the Syndicate.

Joey grinned at him. "Do you really think my uncles in Sicily made pasta?"

Bulldog's dream was within reach. Joey thought he was big enough and probably dumb enough to be useful, then probably easy to get rid of, if necessary.

In a short time, Mr. Abner Tanner, the Bulldog, was a low-level member of the Atlanta branch of Joey's family, doing whatever they told him to do.

He started playing poker with his new friends on a regular basis — and losing spectacularly on a regular basis, proving to Joey he was plenty dumb – at least when it came to poker. At first, Bulldog would siphon off petty cash from the construction business. But he had to be careful. Princess, his father's longtime secretary, kept an eagle eye on the books. He wished her fat ass would drop dead from a heart attack. The woman had to weigh 300 pounds. Bulldog had no idea why her parents named her that.

Didn't know, didn't care. The bitch had a mean streak a mile wide, but she adored his father.

Joey's family owned Caranuto's, a chain of successful Italian restaurants scattered around the city, and they were making plans to expand throughout the Southeast. Nobody knew the restaurants were money laundering operations. In addition to making homemade pasta, they were running guns and drugs from New York to Florida.

In the beginning, Bulldog was able to keep his illegal entanglements from Mindy. Then one night, "The Wise Guys" — as they called themselves — insisted on coming to Bulldog and Mindy's to play poker.

Bulldog's dad had moved the trailer to another job site after the marriage. He also changed the locks, so that location was a no-go.

Bulldog decided he had no choice but to play host.

The guys, all a generation older than Bulldog and Mindy, sat down to play.

Mindy had just come off a 12-hour shift at the hospital. She greeted the men with her usual Southern manners, then went to take a long bath and go to bed. She had another early shift the next morning.

The cards didn't favor Bulldog. He emptied his wallet, the cash from the safe in the guest bedroom, then went into Mindy's purse, which she always left in the kitchen, and snatched all her cash. The gangsters let him play on until his debt amounted to just over two grand. When his friends asked how he was going to settle up, he told them he had no more cash in the house.

"I can pay you over time."

"No," said Guido — his real name — the local Mafia leader. He had a revolting laugh.

Then Carmine stood up. "Go into the bedroom and get your wife. Tell her to put on make-up and her most expensive lingerie and come and join the party."

"I can't do that. She's got another early shift in the morning."

"You better," Carmine said, laughing.

"We'll make it easy for her," Guido said. "Marty over there can mix up a special little cocktail for her. It won't hurt her, and she won't remember anything in the morning but a good time."

Bulldog's shoulders slumped. He agreed and padded back to the bedroom and gently woke Mindy, who always slept like a log. He explained what she had to do, then gave her the cocktail to drink, telling her it was only vodka to make her relax a little.

Mindy didn't want to drink the cocktail or join the party, but Bulldog told her it was Marty's specialty, mixed just for her. Mindy began to realize what was going on — neither she nor her husband had a choice about what was going on in their own home and she was terrified.

Mindy downed the cocktail in one swallow, hoping to pass out, hoping the drink was drugged, and put on the long, black satin gown and sheer black robe she'd bought for their wedding night. The satin hugged all her curves and left little to the imagination. They rejoined the group, and Mindy had a feeling she'd never experienced. She felt totally relaxed. She wasn't a big drinker and prayed for oblivion.

"You're smart to play ball," Guido said to Bulldog. He,

Carmine and Marty all laughed, but Bulldog was flushed and breathing heavily.

Bulldog didn't feel smart. He was scared shitless, and wanted to hide it for Mindy's sake, but he just couldn't.

Mindy was feeling the full effect of Marty's cocktail as one of the guys turned on music and asked Mindy to dance. She did so with a sexual energy she'd never felt before. She felt uninhibited and couldn't gather her thoughts. She danced, then went over and sat on one lap, and then another. She felt like she was spinning.

Marty said, "Hey little lady, you're all right. Show us your bedroom."

"Now wait just a second," Bulldog said. "This has gone far enough."

Guido nodded at Marty, who knocked the hell out of Bulldog with the help of Rocco, who hadn't uttered a sound the whole night. Guido and Rocco brought out some rope and tied Bulldog to a heavy kitchen chair.

Carmine said again, "Show us your bedroom, pretty lady."
"It's right down the hall, fellas."

The four winked at each other and followed Mindy down the hall. Dazed, Bulldog heard their bedroom door lock. He thought about screaming but he couldn't get his breath and stayed silent. Who knows what they might do to Mindy if he did?

An hour later — Bulldog knew how much time had passed because he could see the Kitty Kat kitchen clock, its tail ticking back and forth, back and forth — Carmine and Guido came out of the bedroom. Mindy and Marty were not with them.

Bulldog panicked. What had happened to his wife? He kept quiet, fearful of what they'd do to him — and to her. Then he heard the sound of the shower, and Marty came and stood outside the bathroom. After what seemed like forever, the water went off. A few minutes after that, Marty came down the hall. He joined Guido, Carmine, and Rocco, who by this time were putting on their fake leather jackets and joking with one another.

"Thanks for being a team player," Guido told Bulldog as the others untied the younger man. "You're going to do well in our organization. Just keep doing what we say, and make sure your wife is always available for poker night."

The Wise Guys laughed as they went out the door. Bulldog sat still for a few moments until he heard the motor of their Cadillac roar to life outside the window. As the engine sound faded in the distance, Bulldog raced into the bedroom. Mindy was sound asleep in the cotton nightgown she always wore. Her hair was still wet. Bulldog wasn't a religious man, but he prayed that she wouldn't remember a thing when she woke up.

But she did remember, though not clearly. She shuddered at the thought of what had happened to her, and her brain was clear enough to understand why.

Bulldog. Bully.

She didn't fully understand the depth of what her husband was involved in. It didn't seem possible that he could be so heavily involved in gambling that it brought that horror into their home.

She began to understand her sister's objections to Bulldog,

and she decided it was time to find out more.

He behaved like a beaten puppy for a few days but said absolutely nothing to her. Mostly he avoided her. It only made her resentment grow. She started thinking of ways to get away from him and the awful place her home had become.

The decline

Mandy didn't like Bulldog from the start and vice versa. She saw right through him. For the life of her, Mandy couldn't see what her twin saw in him. She was the one who started calling him Bully. He was nothing like the guys Mindy dated in high school.

Mandy knew their parents — retired and living in Florida — would not be amused. Mindy knew it, too, and put off their meeting as long as possible.

Bulldog didn't even ask her about it. She figured it was because he was estranged from his mother and didn't get along with his father, even though they worked together.

That's the reason Bulldog was assistant project manager, more or less a title his father made up. What it meant was that he spent his days driving from site to site, making sure jobs were being accomplished his father's way. Each morning, he got a list of instructions from Princess and set out for the day.

Bulldog had to be at the construction office every morning by 6 a.m., but he got off by 2 p.m. The crews knocked off an hour later. The supervisors had the day wrapped up by then, and they no longer needed him. That allowed time for him to go and drink for at least three hours before it was time to go home.

That's what he did before he married Mindy, and he saw no reason to change his schedule since she worked 12-hour days. Problem was, Mindy only worked three days a week, so, dammit, she did expect him home by 2:30 on her days off. So as not to raise her suspicions, he reluctantly changed. Hell, why not? They were newlyweds. The sex was fantastic. He'd never met a more enthusiastic lover. Everything was new to her — she wanted to try it all and they did. Bulldog was one happy man.

Until he wasn't.

Bulldog married Mindy in large part because he knew she would make lots of money as a nurse, and he could slack off even more at the construction company.

He basically cruised around to different job sites. Thank God his father had hired good onsite supervisors. Barry Tanner knew deep down his son was no count. He couldn't understand why. He blamed his ex-wife for being too soft on him. That was the main reason he and Linda eventually divorced.

Six months after Bulldog and Mindy's wedding, when Mindy was paying their bills, she noticed some odd charges on their shared credit card. Bulldog hemmed and hawed, finally admitting he was having some problems with gambling.

"I'm sorry, baby. Just stay with me. Don't leave me. I can stop anytime. I promise I'll join Gamblers Anonymous."

He didn't. He was a pro at throwing promises out with no intention of actually doing anything.

A year in, he became more and more paranoid. He told Mindy he wanted her to quit work and keep his books. He didn't want her to see her parents or twin sister any longer. He thought they were out to get him. True, they disliked Bulldog from day one, but they were never out to get him.

Since his part of the business wasn't all that busy, Mindy convinced him she could continue working her 12-hour shifts three days a week and do his accounting. That way he wouldn't have to hire anyone. She'd learned quickly that her husband was a cheapskate. And after the poker game, she just didn't trust him.

Simultaneously, she was offered to switch to the night shift on weekends. It was so much more money considering the differential for weekend and night work. When they first married, Bulldog made her sign her paychecks over to him. When she switched jobs, she told him her new supervisor said this was not possible, that she'd be paid by direct deposit. This wasn't true, but Mindy had decided to start a fund to leave the marriage.

Bulldog was suspicious but accepted the check she wrote him each payday.

"You know, I make less money now because it's fewer hours," she lied to him. He looked at her dumbly. He bought it — he was too wrapped up with The Family to ask any questions. It didn't take Mindy long to save enough money to start a new life.

One Sunday morning, when she knew Bulldog would be sleeping off his Saturday-night hangover in the guest bedroom, Mindy arranged to meet her sister for coffee. She told Mandy about her plans to leave town the next day. She'd accepted a nursing position at Duke University Hospital in Durham, North Carolina.

Mandy was upset, but knew it was for the best. She hugged her sister tight and promised to come see her once she got settled into her apartment. The next day, after Bulldog left for work, Mindy grabbed her bag of toiletries, emptied her jewelry box in a plastic bag, and left the townhouse she once loved for the last time. She hated every inch of it now. The week before, she'd put her biggest suitcase in the back of her Jeep Cherokee. Bulldog always drove his Ford 350 pickup — with its annoying diesel engine — so he never noticed.

Mindy breathed a sigh of relief hours later when she saw the "Welcome to North Carolina" sign.

Mindy canceled their shared credit card. Bulldog didn't know about her checking account, but she closed it before she left town. She didn't dare get another credit card. She took plenty of cash. She figured by the time Bulldog found out where she was — if he found out — she'd be safe. She had to wait a year until she could file for divorce, and until then wanted as little a paper trail as possible.

Mindy's parents agreed to rent the Durham apartment for her under a newly formed corporation, and she paid the corporation for rent and utilities. She paid cash for everything else. It took a little while to get the hang of it, but before long she was a pro, keeping money for groceries, clothes, and incidentals in separate envelopes.

Eventually, she no longer felt the need to constantly look over her shoulder. She traded cars, just to be on the safe side, and got a great deal for her nearly new Cherokee. She bought a small Toyota — with cash — to help her save money on gas, even though her new commute was pretty short. If she didn't work nights, she could have easily walked to work. She put the vehicle title in the corporation's name, just in case. She was too embarrassed to tell her parents the whole story.

"He's lazy," she said, "and he drinks too much and likes to gamble. I just want to get away and start over. You were right about him all along," she told them. Her mother knew there had to be more, but she didn't press. She just wanted her girl to be safe.

Mindy didn't give it a second thought the next spring when she filed her taxes.

Huge mistake.

Not long after Mindy left town, Bulldog's gambling spiraled out of control. The IRS seized his part of his father's company to pay his taxes and gambling debts. Bulldog decided he wasn't going down alone. He told the company's CPA to find Mindy. She was so straight, he knew there was no way she would skip paying taxes. He also told the CPA that Mindy was the one addicted to gambling, that this was all her fault, and unbeknownst to him, she'd cooked his books.

His father wanted nothing to do with the mess his idiot son had created. It had already cost him a boatload, so he pushed Bulldog to do anything he could to get out of trouble.

The Sunday morning after Bulldog made his deal in Atlanta, there were two IRS agents waiting for Mindy in Durham when she got home from work. By then, Bulldog had cut a deal with the local district attorney and ended up serving five years' supervised probation. Mindy protested the ridiculous charges, but the agents said her behavior, leaving the home, covering her trail, was obviously suspicious. Because she'd isolated herself to keep Bulldog from finding her, she didn't have anyone who knew her well enough to stand up for her. Bulldog was too slick a liar, and knew some things through The Family that certain officials didn't want known at all.

She simply followed the agents to their unmarked car.

Mindy got five years in prison for tax evasion. Even though her "crime" took place in Georgia, she was sent to Women's Prison in Raleigh since she was now a North Carolina resident. The Georgia district attorney was fine with that, and waived extradition.

Just like Judge Victor Adams understood Bob's plight, Mindy's judge knew that her ex-husband had set her up. He and the Georgia DA were classmates at Wake Forest Law

School. They'd kept in touch.

Like Adams, Judge Phillip Lassiter knew it was moot to recuse himself. He knew there was no way that poor girl would be found innocent. Her sleazy ex-husband had seen to that.

And Lassiter had heard things about an ongoing fraud investigation that Abner Tanner might be involved in. Lassiter could not afford to interfere with that.

Bulldog, though, was headed for a different fate. Two years into Mindy's prison sentence, some of The Family's newly hired lowlifes killed Bulldog over a debt he couldn't pay. After Mindy had left him, he'd started going to the track. He had borrowed money from the Mob's in-house loan shark at 50 percent interest. He was desperate, but he knew the bet was "a sure thing." Or so the Mob's insider at the track told him.

Black Fury, the favorite, was to be doped that night by one of the Mob lackeys to throw the race. Bulldog bet on the second horse, Big Thunder, to be the winner. He felt a big payday coming, which he desperately needed. Unfortunately, the man who tried to dope the horse was caught before the race started.

Black Fury won — and Bulldog lost his life.

Prison life

It didn't take Bob long to get into the prison routine. The schedule was rigid — breakfast, lunch, dinner, yard time, lights out. He had his janitorial schedule and spent time in the library tutoring inmates for their GED and ESL course work. With his remaining time, which wasn't much, he researched information about his formula. His father faithfully sent every book Bob requested. Even though he was in prison, it wasn't that difficult at first, as he lived and worked in the hospital wing. He kept his head down.

That was exactly what attracted the attention of some of the other inmates who thought the new guy was getting way too many breaks. Rumors ran throughout the prison, changing with every telling. Everyone was trying to find a way to get ahead, no matter what it took.

A couple of guys figured Bob was the warden's pet. They started to show up at the infirmary, watching Bob as he cleaned, dropping filth on the floors, kicking the mop out of his hand.

Then they started coming to the GED classes, asking questions that made Bob uncomfortable. "Bobby Boy, what you do to the warden?" the one called Long Neck asked. Everyone laughed. Bob didn't answer. Later, a big, but limping guy called Monkey said, "I heard you made some promises you can't keep. You need more practice!"

Bob knew that word of his research would bring questions, at least, but he hadn't really thought through how a bunch of frustrated men would turn against him.

When they started following him to the library and knocking his books to the floor or playing keep-away with them, he didn't say anything to the warden. He laughed at their endless obscene jokes, slapped them on the back as hard as they slapped him.

When he said he was getting nowhere with his idea, they teased him even more about it. He began to watch everyone around him, wondering what the next move would be.

He told no one, hoping that the whole thing would be forgotten, that someone new would divert their attention, in time. But he was very alone.

Long Neck and Monkey made Bob their project, spitting in his food, bumping into him so hard he fell a couple times. When Monkey reached to pick him up, his grip left painful bruises. The verbal harassment caught on with some of the other inmates, who thought they were very funny.

Bob had some consolation. Bill wrote his son faithfully every week. He also had letters from Cotton, Hazel, Judge Adams, the ladies from the church prison ministry, Big John, Mr. and Mrs. Jackson, Woodberry classmates, a couple of his Duke fraternity brothers, and Joe Mason from the landscape team. Their letters reflected their personalities. Cotton's, for example, were just a few lines, brief and to the point. The prison ministry ladies sent beautiful cards, saying they were constantly praying for him. Bob believed them. The fraternity brothers kept things light, filling him in on their lives and their children's activities, as if he were away at summer camp. Joe told him what he was planting in the gardens depending on the season, and the new annuals and recently released tulip bulbs he was trying.

Every letter was kind and upbeat and made Bob realize how lucky he was — no matter where he was. Reading and re-reading the letters calmed him somewhat in the evenings — the loneliest time of day for inmates is between supper and lights out at 10. He was glad to know that his friends and family "on the outside" hadn't forgotten him and believed him.

One of the guards told Bob at mail call that he received the most mail of any inmate at Central Prison. But getting all that mail just drew more attention to him from lonely and abandoned inmates. Someone stole his collection of supportive letters one day during supper time. Bob determined he would read and then destroy all future notes. Again, he did not report the theft to anyone.

It was such a fragile balancing act, keeping his cool, following orders, staying quiet. Guilty or not, Bob was being punished.

At least he earned the correction officers' respect with politeness and cooperation. He always answered their questions with "Yes, sir" or "No, sir." He didn't speak unless they spoke first. After he shared his story with them, they at least felt sorry for him, even if they didn't necessarily believe he was innocent.

That still made him feel good. He had the best relationship possible with the officers in the hospital wing.

That made him smile. It made his enemies think of ways to knock him down a few notches. And one day during exercises, Long Neck and Monkey and a couple others decided Bob would be their personal football. A pileup of guys playing football was usually ignored. It was a good way for them to get rid of some of their aggression. Better to do it in the yard.

Bob ended up on the bottom of the pile, bruised, scraped, gasping for a clean breath. He figured he had one or more broken ribs. He had a bloody nose and lip, maybe a loose tooth. The gang left him in the dirt, laughing as they walked away. Bob decided to stay put for a while. Moving was going to hurt like hell.

"Okay, buddy, get up. Time to go back to your cell," the guard said, prodding Bob on the shoulder with his foot. "Come on. Up!"

Bob turned his head, and the officer saw the blood. He got a pair of gloves from his pocket, put them on and reached out a hand to Bob.

He did have 2 broken ribs, a large gash on his shin, numerous bruises, a broken thumb, dislocated nose and busted lip. When officers questioned him, he said little. "All I know is we were playing football, and I was on the bad end of a tackle. The guys on top of me must have had it pretty bad, too."

They knew he was lying, and they understood why.
The doctor decided Bob should stay the night in the infirmary and made it clear to the guards no visitors were allowed.

When he woke the next morning, aching all over, Bob first thanked God that his injuries weren't worse. He realized that being quiet was not helping. And spilling the beans wouldn't either. He had to be smarter than they were. He had to develop some sort of skill to counteract the situation.

He declined his exercise period that day, going to the relative safety of his cell. He did not need a repeat performance. He did show up for supper in the cafeteria, bandaged, bruises clearly visible. He'd been so determined to rise above his condition that he didn't have any prison buddies. That was one of the first things he needed to do, have a fellow prisoner on his side. He needed to learn a way to defend himself, physically. He had to adjust his attitude. He wasn't guilty, but 99 percent of the other men thought they weren't guilty, either. He had to factor that in. He had to realize he was without position, easy money or family status. He was beginning to understand what humility felt like.

Mindy in prison

For Mindy, the thought of prison was terrifying. It brought up the awful memories of that horrible night when Bulldog's "payment" for losing poker was her body – even drugged, she remembered enough of what happened to have a mild panic attack when reminded.

Her attorney told her that she had committed a financial crime, not a violent one, and would likely be housed with similar offenders. In her weaker moments, she wished she had committed a violent crime against those evil men.

She looked down at the floor during her intake, not wanting to make eye contact, but during her interview, she recognized a kinder tone of voice.

Officer K'Shelle Johnson was about Mindy's age, she guessed. She was formal and firm, then started asking questions.

“Look up, Tanner. Look me in the eye and tell me your story.”

Mindy did look up and gathered herself. “I did not cheat the IRS in any way. My husband got involved with the Mob and got deeply into debt.” Then she described what she could about that night and noticed the officer wince. Mindy felt a little shaky, but she went on. “I couldn’t stay with him. I couldn’t trust him. I realized that everything he told me was a lie. So I did what I had to do to get away from him. I wanted to make myself as invisible as possible because I did not want him, or the Mob, to find me. The only thing I wanted to do was start my life over, focus on my career and rebuild some sort of normal.
By filing taxes, I was doing the right thing. I was honest, and that bastard – excuse me – turned it around on me.”

Johnson was quiet for a few moments, looking at Mindy, making sure they maintained eye contact.

“Your employer did not support you?”

“My direct supervisor believed me, but that was not enough for the courts.”

She had immediately lost her job. She didn’t know what would happen if – when – she got out of prison.

“It’s a pretty wild story,” Johnson said. “But I saw you go pale and heard your mouth dry up when you talked about those men. If you keep your wits about you, do as you’re told, you’ll survive this place. If you have the skills you say, we’ll put you to work. Stay away from the troublemakers, keep yourself to yourself. How’d you like to work in the infirmary part time?”

Mindy felt some relief. She wasn’t sure what the officer

believed, but she hadn't laughed her off. Having a chance to work made a huge difference.

She had felt so alone when she was arrested, but now, her sister Mandy wrote to her regularly, as did her parents. Her mother's church circle sent Mindy cards and various items allowed by the rules. Her supervisor at the hospital even wrote a few times. It seemed that she and her co-workers were sympathetic to her after finding out more about Mindy's past.

Mindy was not like Bob during her time in prison. She made no attempt to ingratiate herself with anyone. She figured if she just took one day at a time and kept her mouth shut, she might survive.

But Mindy was pretty, and her quiet demeanor brought its own kind of attention. Her fellow inmates provoked her constantly, trying to make her angry, get her to talk or lash back.

Mindy was not a church goer, but she talked to God every day, asking for mercy, pleading for protection. It was as if she'd been thrown back into Bulldog's lies and crimes all over again. She had nightmares. She lost weight and energy. She knew these were signs of depression, and that not eating was making her weak, possibly anemic. Jessica Snyder, the nurse practitioner at the infirmary, noticed, too, and sat down to talk to her.

"Mindy, I don't care if you're guilty or innocent, but I do know your sentence is not that long. You won't be around to see freedom if you keep this up."

Mindy started crying, and shivering.

"Come on, we've got to fix this, or they'll send you to

Broughton and you do not want to spend five years there, trust me."

Mindy took an offered tissue and told her story with the fewest details possible.

"Almost every woman in this prison has a story of abuse. And then, it just takes a different form once they get here. Some of them survive by doing the same to someone else. Some shut down, only to be victimized. But here, we talk about it. We treat what we can. I can refer you to a counselor. Many of the women here get counseling. It's not as often as we'd like, it's not always an answer, but it can help. What do you think?"

"I've tried so hard not to talk about it. It seemed better to bury it and try to forget. I was ready to move on until ..."

Jessica could see the anger wash over Mindy, and she held up her hand, "Stop."

Mindy exhaled, her face flushed.

"Here's my prescription – you must eat. You know that. And I will give you an antihistamine that will make you sleepy. You'll have to come here every day to get it. Then I'll get you in to see Patti Ross, she's the best counselor available here."

"Thank you, Ms. Snyder."

"And another thing. There are women here very much like you, just as scared and angry. I'll tell you who they are. You seek them out. There is safety – and healing – in numbers."

Mindy, still shaky, made an effort to eat. She pretended the food was a gourmet meal at a quiet restaurant. She kept saying, "Mind over matter, mind over matter."

Slowly, a few women approached her in different places around the prison. Jessica Snyder was right – there were plenty of women like Mindy. They found strength in each other. Mindy kept up with the nursing journals, which gave her more focus; maybe she could pick up her career when she was free. She would not let Bulldog destroy her. She remembered a phrase her father had used, "The greatest revenge is success."

Counselor Patti had too many patients with too many needs. She'd learned after about a year contracting with the prison system that she had to work smarter, not harder. She needed a mentoring group at the prison, women who could reach out and help each other.

She listened to Mindy's story. Obviously, she had post-traumatic stress syndrome. But she had enough smarts to get away from her abuser. Her nursing career meant she was capable of and willing to help others. Patti thought Mindy could be a mentor to another inmate. That would increase her own coping skills and make her feel more confident. At this point, Mindy had hit rock bottom. Patti could see she wanted a way up and out.

"Mindy," she said one day after a group session, "I think you have some very special skills which we can tap into."

"Me?"

"Yes. I know you are traumatized, but I'm also thinking you're pretty strong, and that you picked a caring profession.

"I always wanted to be a nurse and help people, ever since I was a little girl."

"I think there's something we can do here to help you, which will in turn help others. You know this can be a very scary place; it's a cauldron of emotions and hurts like yours. I want you to consider being a mentor to one of your sister inmates."

Mindy said nothing at first. She looked away and picked at her uniform. "I can barely help myself."

"But you are smart enough to understand that helping others IS helping yourself. You focus on their needs, and that makes you feel better. I'm sure you learned that in school."

Mindy did know that. It was something her mother had said to her long ago. Her school guidance counselor had praised Mindy for reaching out to other students. Her nurse training had emphasized that. Then she'd learned to find the line between caring and becoming overwrought over someone's problems.

"What would I need to do," she asked Patti.

"I'm going to match you with someone. All you have to do is be there for them. Have meals with her, let her tell her story. The two of you can work on solutions. Having support like that will make you both stronger."

Mindy sighed, swallowed hard. "I guess it would be okay to try. I know I don't want to live like this anymore."

A couple of weeks later, after another group session, Patti introduced Mindy to Erin. Erin had abusive parents who used her in a money-laundering scam, setting her up in a small business. The scheme had cost Erin everything – her dreams of being her own boss, of providing a service for others and of marrying her boyfriend, who ended up being partners with her parents. Everything was gone. She felt completely alone.

At least Mindy had a supportive family. She had hopes of returning to nursing in some capacity, and she was likely never marrying again.

Erin was easy to talk to. Mindy immediately felt how lonely and lost she was. She was slightly younger than Mindy, so she had even more to look forward to. But because she was timid and battle-scarred, Erin was also a target for the bullies. Mindy had been, too. But in the time after Bulldog, she'd learned self-defense techniques. She was physically stronger, even if her mind wasn't there yet.

Counselor Patti was right. Helping Erin was good for Mindy. She realized what she needed to do to cope with her situation as she and Erin talked. Mindy needed to be strong for her friend; she needed to be stronger for herself. Patti asked Mindy to help another inmate, too. The three of them formed a bond, made plans for their futures, fought the little daily battles of prison life. Mindy was hungry again. She worked out harder, relying on her old training, and the other women joined her. Physical activity was a great way to relieve stress and manage aggression. Patti felt a sense of relief that these women, at least, weren't giving up – that they could face the challenges ahead.

Bob and Mindy meet

The five-year prison sentences for Bob and Mindy eventually passed. They were released with clean records and high hopes for a new life.

It's hard to say which one learned more. Mindy felt so much stronger and even thought about getting a counseling degree.

Stripped of most privileges, Bob finally understood the value of humility. He was around people who didn't get a full scholarship, didn't have a private plane. They struggled for success and honor. They made mistakes and paid for them. Bob better understood the consequences, and he thanked God, his father and Lucy Athena.

After their releases, they joined the Transitional Aftercare Network (TAN) to help inmates move from incarceration and rejoin society at large.

They met at the first TAN meeting in Raleigh. At first, Bob thought Mindy was a volunteer since she was serving coffee. When the meeting started, she sat down next to him. She was gorgeous, with blue eyes and light brown hair. He couldn't believe she'd been in prison.

At the break, he introduced himself. While chatting, they realized their stories were eerily similar. Although Mindy was extremely cautious, by the end of the meeting, they were friends. Mindy thought Bob could be helpful as she restarted her career.

As they saw more of each other, both at meetings and in the real world, Bob was impressed that Mindy had kept up with the latest developments in nursing, and at her calm confidence. Mindy saw that Bob was ambitious and had a promising support system.

Mindy literally had nothing to go back to in Durham. The IRS had seized everything. She couldn't visit her parents or her sister because she could not leave the state.

Bob had The Retreat. He was talking to his father about what he would do and mentioned meeting Mindy.

"Oh, Bob, she isn't one of those women, is she?" Bill asked.

"Dad, she is the total opposite. You'd like her. She has nowhere to go back to, so ..."

"Are you moving too quickly," Bill asked.

"I don't want to lose any more time. I'm sure she can help me with my research. I want to give her an option."

Bill said he would clean up the small cabin on the property. "Then it's up to you."

Mindy was reluctant at first. She went to the public library to see what she could find out about the Hendersons. Bob arranged a phone call with Bill, and Mindy decided it was worth a chance. Once she restored her nursing credentials, she could move.

Once they were both at The Retreat, Mindy realized how lucky she was. Bob's father was very protective of her, making sure she was comfortable and settled. He was thinking of his daughter Liz. Maybe Mindy wouldn't mind a little pampering.

Bob and Mindy became closer, more than friends, after a short time. It had been a long five years, and each one needed someone they could trust.

Photo by Sean Meyers Photography

Where do we go from here?

Once Bob's grandfather decided to divest from his cotton crop in 1952, he chose to plant wheat, corn, and soybeans. Hugh never did anything halfway. He thoroughly researched the new crops, and got help and advice from Bill's friend Richard and his father.

He joined all the different brokers exchange organizations, along with national and international commodities and agricultural groups. In the international group, he met a farmer from Argentina. Their stories were almost parallel. They'd grown up poor, but eventually amassed a great deal of land.

Felipe Hernandez-Garcia and Hugh hit it off from the start, since they had so much in common. At the end of the first meeting, Felipe extended an invitation to Hugh and Bill to come for a visit. He sent his private plane for them in the summer of 1953.

Hugh and Bill reciprocated by inviting Felipe to come to The Retreat the next summer, even though they didn't have a plane capable of flying that distance. That was okay with Felipe. He flew up in his own plane, a brand-new Beechcraft Bonanza.

Thus began a long and fruitful friendship between the two families. Son Julio eventually took over Felipe's farming operations. Bill and Bob went to Argentina twice when Bob was home from Duke. By then, Julio was his country's largest soybean producer. He urged Bill to convert from soybeans, wheat, and corn to exclusively rotating soybeans and corn, growing only enough wheat for the Black Angus beef cattle and the family's horses. One bushel of soybeans is equal to two bushels of corn in value, as there's more protein in soybeans. Ever the savvy businessman, Bill thought the plan made sense.

Julio wrote to Bob while he was in prison. When he got out, Bob wrote to ask if Julio could help him with the management of a manufacturing facility. Bob was ready to test his drug, and he hoped it wouldn't be long before he could take it to market. In South America, he wouldn't have to go through a decade-long FDA approval process. He still wanted to be as careful as possible and closely monitor any side effects. Because of the drug combinations he was using, his hunch was there would be none.

Julio responded immediately and said he'd be glad to help in any way. He said he always thought so much of Bill and Hugh.

After much scientific analysis — and more than a little prayer — Bob decided to be Patient Zero. If everything turned out well with his tests, he'd ask some close associates to participate.

Two of his former partners had reached out to him after his release from prison to say they finally understood some of what happened, and that Bob was probably not a criminal but a victim. They volunteered to help him with development of the medication. He'd also received a recent letter from Warden Dixon, reminding Bob of his interest. A couple of the correction officers at Central Prison said they'd help, too. The rest of the volunteers included some of his traveling buddies from Europe, Woodberry classmates, and former frat brothers. It was a small pool to start, but Bob figured if this drug worked in preliminary trials, he'd have a lot more men clamoring to sign up for additional trials once it went public.

Then he'd start testing a slightly different formula for women. That might take a little more convincing — but maybe not — he had a good woman by his side. Bob thanked God he was able to get his medical license back.

The women's side

"Poor Bob, bless his heart," Mindy thought. "You'd think being a urologist he'd have some idea about women's bodies, but because of his bad marriage and the early death of his sister, he doesn't know their minds." Women wanted to be just as sexually satisfied as men, but they had been raised not to speak up, not to express interest.

The two of them were going to change that.

They knew from preliminary research that you can't just make a pink pill instead of a blue pill and call it done. There's a lot more to the plumbing, as Dr. Young, one of the partners who was supporting Bob, always said.

Based on Bob and Mindy's focus groups, women told her they needed a formula that naturally stimulated their libido and made intercourse more comfortable. In addition, women approaching menopause and beyond didn't sleep that well. Caffeine was a no-no. Dryness and overall exhaustion were not a winning combination for a night of passion.

After months of testing — the men's formula had been completed — they came up with an estrogen gel with proprietary botanical ingredients. The women's Endless Spring packaging also came with a vial of rosemary essential oil, known to boost the desire for activity. Women — or their partners — smoothed a couple drops on both sides of the neck, bringing about alertness through aromatherapy with no side effects.

After rounds of testing showed no issues, they were ready to take Endless Spring public. With their shared recent histories, they just weren't sure of the best path.

A fresh start

Mindy and Bob decided to move to Argentina at the end of 1987. They were ready for a fresh start. Julio encouraged them to move near La Plata. It was the capital city of the Buenos Aires province, but not as crowded as the larger city itself. Through Julio's connections, they soon found a furnished villa near the sea, and an abandoned factory they could easily convert to manufacturing space.

The villa had plenty of land around it. After five years in prison, they wanted wide-open spaces. Bob had his FAA pilot's license validated by the Argentine authorities to avoid any problems if he needed to fly to find supplies or bring in advisors.

Julio had gone to college with the president of Argentina. That's how Mindy and Bob met Javier Gonzalez. They were invited to numerous dinners at the presidential residence with Gonzalez and his glamorous wife, Angelica. People were always fascinated by expats. They didn't mind being shown off — it gave them many personal and professional connections in their newly adopted country.

The Ledford Brothers sell out

While Bob was away, Bill kept busy with The Retreat, his dogs, and his other business interests. He knew his son was doing well, but still, it kept his mind off things. Bill never admitted it to him, but Bob's time in prison was a long five years for him.

One day, Bill had a call from Cotton, asking if he and Bird Dog could come for a visit. He was happy to hear from him, because he missed his son so much.

In Bill's study, the two of them got right down to business after the usual pleasantries. It was their way. They were mountain men not fond of idle chitchat.

Their father and grandfather had died within a year of each other, and the brothers decided they were ready to get out of the moonshine business. Heart disease ran in their family. The men typically died young, and Cotton and Bird Dog didn't want to be another statistic. They'd vowed to start taking better care of themselves, and the inherent stress of their chosen career was starting to get the better of them, they could tell.

Bill mulled it over with them. He'd already set them up with a legitimate dairy farm years before.

"Let's just end it," Bill told them. "It's not worth the risk anymore. We're all getting older."

The vote was unanimous.

Bill had helped Cotton and Bird Dog grow their money through a diversified portfolio of conservative, dividend-paying, blue chip stocks. His personal money manager also managed their accounts. They were in a position to hire someone to manage the dairy farm.

Bill sold the mom-and-pop stores to a grocery chain owner who wanted to modernize them. Frank Butler, CEO of Butler's Supermarkets, had built up a chain of five supermarkets in western North Carolina. Frank started in the grocery business as a bag boy and stocker. He bought his first store with an inheritance from a grandfather who was killed when a drunk driver hit him on Highway 421 near Wilkesboro on his way home to Piney Creek. Because his parents died before his grandfather, Frank got a substantial insurance settlement, and with it, he bought his very first store.

Frank had clean stores, good products, and offered no credit. He brought grocery shopping into the 20th century. In a couple of years, he built another store, and another, and another. He decided it was time to approach Bill, a longtime acquaintance.

Bill's stores were well-loved but dated, old-timey and old-fashioned. They had a solid base of customers who loved their nostalgic vibe. It had worked well for many years, and Bill saw no reason to change it. But Frank wanted control in the mountains to meet growing demand. What he would do with these stores was his business, not Bill's.

Frank and Bill met — just one-on-one, no attorneys present — negotiated the sale, and shook hands. Frank financed the deal through Bill, and he sold the grocery stores to him. It was an easy transaction, and they toasted each other with a glass of The Reserve whiskey.

Bill could realize his dream to expand the airstrip at The Retreat and enlarge the hangar. Sure, it was a splurge, but now he had plenty of disposable income.

Construction complete, Bill bought a King Air turboprop plane. He wanted Bob to have first-class transportation to fly back and forth to Argentina.

When it was all said and done, Bill's estate was worth $30 million. His father Hugh was worth $50 million when he died. Pretty good for two country boys who started as mill workers. Bill had made money with his father in the commodities business.

Bill would help Bob any way he could, but he wanted him to make his own way in the world. He need not have worried. Bob and Mindy built their fortune in Argentina.

A dream finally realized

Before Bob made the move to South America, Bill thought it would be a good idea for Mindy to take flying lessons, and Bob agreed. She was a natural and passed her tests with flying colors, as they say. It was good to have a co-pilot in the plane and in his life, Bob thought.

They got to know President and Mrs. Gonzalez well. They gave Bob and Mindy a beautiful German Shepherd Dog. She was a loyal guard dog. She only knew German commands, so Mindy and Bob took extensive training to learn to handle her. Some days Bob felt like the dog was smarter than they were. Elke was amazing. Indeed, Bob and Mindy felt safer with her around the compound.

President Gonzalez gave them other gifts, too — AR-15 assault rifles with a duffel bag full of loaded magazines. The country was stable when they arrived, but the president knew things could shift, as had happened so many times before.

At this point, seven coups d'etat had rocked the nation in 1930, 1943, 1955, 1962, 1966, 1976, and as recently as 1981. It was almost as if the clock was ticking for the next one.

The first four set up temporary dictators, while the fifth and sixth brought a more permanent bureaucratic-authoritarian state. The coups of 1976 and '81 had involved terrorism. Argentine citizens lost many of their rights, while other Argentinians simply disappeared, and remain unaccounted for.

Through the years of turmoil, various military governments were formed, but there was constant change and upheaval. For the last few years, the country had been trying to establish a Democracy but was still plagued by hardliners and those who wanted revenge for atrocities committed during the coups.

Gonzalez told Bob and Mindy there might come a day when they would need to leave the country at a moment's notice. He urged them to have go-bags packed and the plane fully fueled and ready.

Mindy and Bob took his advice and prepared. Mindy had insisted that Bob stay in shape. She worked out daily and they created a self-defense routine. It made Mindy feel much stronger. Foreigners were easy targets for thefts and useful as hostages should unrest develop. After dealing with her ex-husband – and the Mob – she had learned to take care of herself, no matter what. Bob knew she loved him, and he loved her, but she told him early in their relationship that she'd never be dependent on a man again. He respected that.

The thought of another unjust imprisonment was plenty of motivation to stay alert and aware.
They were true partners.

The development of the male and female versions of the treatment went well. Plenty of people wanted jobs, and they told their friends about the product, bringing more volunteers for testing. One thing Bob and Mindy were confident about was the development of their line. Success is a beautiful thing.

While things were going well in Argentina, they decided to make their relationship official. President and Mrs. Gonzalez insisted on holding the wedding ceremony at their home, just the four of them, followed by an exquisite dinner. The evening was lovely and intimate, just what they wanted.

The good feelings from that night would become a happy memory. One of many Bob and Mindy held on to as their world was changing yet again.

President Gonzalez was correct in his political forecast. Five years after Bob and Mindy arrived, the political situation started to deteriorate. He called them one night around midnight — late calls never bring good news — and said that he and Angelica were leaving the next day for vacation and invited them to go along. This was a code they'd practiced. Bob told him they'd be glad to meet them at the presidential palace early the next afternoon. None of this was true — they all knew the lines were bugged.

Javier and Angelica fled to Switzerland, where he'd deposited money in bank accounts for years. They survived, although they'd live the rest of their lives in exile. They would miss their home country but were grateful to have an escape.

Mindy and Bob walked out of their villa before dawn. They had spent the night pulling the current batch of drugs from the assembly line with a handful of trusted employees. They could only take so much with them. The rest Bob gave to the plant's manager to sell as he saw fit. They left all the equipment. None of it was proprietary.

The father of another employee had been a munitions expert in the Argentinian army. Bob paid him to set a fire in the plant's storage attic. It would look accidental yet provide enough of a diversion for Mindy and Bob to leave before the police came for them. They knew the doctor and his wife were close friends of the president and first lady.

All along, Bob and Mindy had been loading the plane with cash each time sales reps came from around South America. They were leaving the country with $10 million American. But they could not take their collection of Argentine artwork, some prehistoric, or their carefully selected wine collection. They didn't file a flight plan since they left from a private strip and headed to The Retreat.

A close call

As soon as they heard the sirens, they took off. They were well into the air before the police arrived at the unoccupied villa. They breathed a sigh of relief as the plane climbed higher and higher. They hoped the long flight would be uneventful. Before long, Elke was snoring in her crate.

Bob knew he would have to stop in Brazil for fuel. Then they'd need another refueling spot, and he wasn't so sure of that. The Dominican Republic? He asked Mindy to look at the charts and help find a place. Then they took turns flying the plane. Mindy picked an airport in Brazil, near Fortaleza, to avoid the biggest cities. They were able to refuel quickly, with few questions. They showed their passports and said they'd been doing business in Argentina. The latest coup was working its way into news broadcasts.

Once in the air, Bob looked at the possible stops Mindy had marked for their next refueling. Punta Cana in the

Dominican Republic looked promising. Hours later, Bob noticed the hydraulic light blinking on and off, on and off.

“Dammit,” Bob said, “that means a leak. We have to find a place to land, and fast.” They were approaching the Caribbean. Bob needed a friend on the ground. He might need help fixing the problem. Bob dialed up a frequency he hadn’t used in years.

“Mayday, mayday, emergency landing request on strip 108-Alpha.”

“10-4, your request is granted, Señor Henderson.”

Mindy was confused, but Bob was ecstatic to hear the voice of Alejandro “Alex” Castro (no relation to Fidel). He was grandson of Carlos Castro, who knew Bob’s grandfather, Hugh, when they were in sugar commodities trading. Alex now ran a massive sugar plantation. Even though Cuba was in the “special period” — a devastating economic crisis after the Russians pulled out the year before — Alex was still able to make a great deal of money on the black market.

They were on the ground in minutes. Alex was there to meet them. Bob explained the situation and told him he needed time to fix the hydraulic leak. Because of their extensive preparations Bob made sure he had a fly-away-kit. This tool kit held everything he’d need to repair the hydraulic system temporarily.

Now he just needed time — an hour max. He suggested Mindy get out and stretch her legs and let Elke run. Alex said he would stay close.

“Take your gun,” Bob told her.

She nodded once, then released Elke from her crate. She took off like a shot.

It didn't take long to assess the situation. There was indeed a leak. Bob just needed to switch out some hoses that would hold long enough for them to get home. He got to work. Alex had brought fuel he was pumping into the plane.

"What the hell was that?" Bob cried, hearing gunfire in the distance. He kept working until the sounds grew closer.

"Alex!" he yelled. "What the hell is happening?"

"Keep working, amigo. This is a desperate time for our people. They heard a plane land and they're coming to see what they can steal."

"We have nothing on board," Bob lied. "We had to leave Buenos Aires in a hurry."

"You're Americans. They won't believe you. Keep working. I'll hold them off as long as I can."

"I thought your property was fenced in?"

"It is. Fences won't stop desperation."

Bob needed only a few more minutes to make sure the new hoses were tightly sealed. Alex scanned the area for signs of trouble and tried to hurry the refueling.

The gunfire got closer and closer.

Bob heard Mindy call Elke. Then he heard her give the command to release, and not long after that, the command "Fass!" — German for "attack."

"Oh, no!" Bob said, fearing the worst.

There was nothing he could do but finish the repairs. In a few minutes, he noticed the gunfire had stopped.

“It’s okay, amigo,” Alex called. “Everything is okay!”

The plane was ready. Bob stuck his head out of the entry door to see what was happening and was amazed. There was Elke with a choke hold on a young man, a boy really. His eyes were wide with fear. Elke had him pinned on the ground, still as a statue. Mindy caught Bob’s eye and grinned. She was holding another gun and pointed to the brush around the airstrip.

“Elke and I have everything under control, darling. There’s another one out there, but I think he’s down. Are you ready to go now?”

“Yes, dear. Whatever you say.”

Mindy laughed.

Alex came up with a length of rope. Mindy gave the release word, and Elke gently let go of her prisoner. Then she growled low and slow in the direction where Mindy had pointed. There was no movement, but the sound of someone in distress. Alex tied the rope around the boy, who kept his eyes on Mindy — and her guns.

“This’ll hold him ’til you take off. God be with you, my friends.”

“And with you, Alex,” Bob said, shaking his hand.

Mindy kissed Alex’s cheek, which made him blush. She handed him the extra gun. “I think the other one dropped his weapon in the weeds.” They boarded the plane and took off for the final leg of the long journey.

Return to The Retreat

After the close call in Cuba, they landed as darkness was falling at The Retreat. Bill and his newest retrievers were there to meet them at the strip.

After relieved greetings, Bob and Mindy dropped their bags in Bob's old room and fell into bed. Bill had told them he would take care of Elke, their hero. They slept for hours from the stress of the trip and the long distance in the air.

When they woke, it was late in the afternoon. They smelled something good coming from the kitchen, so they showered and pulled on clean clothes.

Downstairs, they found Bill's companion Nancy in the kitchen grilling steaks on the Jenn-Air. They smelled delicious. It had been many, many hours since they had eaten a real meal.

Bill had found a new relationship. He'd known Nancy in high school but not well since he'd left early to go to Woodberry. She was quite attractive and well educated, having graduated from Meredith College with a degree in art history. During her first marriage, she was a docent at the N.C. Museum of Art in Raleigh. She also loved the outdoors. She loved to hunt and fish, and she was a savvy investor, a member of the local women's philanthropy club. She was perfect for Bill.

Bates Jennings, her first husband, had died of a heart attack several years before. One of Bill's poker buddies suggested he ask Nancy out. They went out to dinner and things progressed from there. At one point, they thought about getting married, because they were truly fond of each other. Nancy had quite a bit of property and a daughter, Nicole, and Bill had The Retreat and Bob.

After consulting their CPAs and attorneys, Bill decided it

was better financially for Nancy that they didn't marry. She agreed. She knew through the grapevine that he was well-off, but she didn't have a greedy bone in her body. She was financially responsible, like him. He didn't know it, and Nancy never mentioned it, but she was actually worth more, because her waterfront land was so much more valuable.

Nancy and Bill remained "steadies" in the parlance of their growing-up days — each other's plus one from now on.

When Nancy had everything on the dining table — she wouldn't let Bob and Mindy lift a finger — they all sat down to a dinner of steak, corn on the cob, fried okra, cucumbers, tomatoes, lima beans, and peach cobbler — all of Bob's favorites.

Not only was Nancy a wonderful companion to Bill, but she was also a fabulous cook. She could whip up a gourmet meal as easily as she could assemble a simple summer supper from farmers' market delights.

As Bob and Mindy thanked her for the food, she explained her skills.

"I love cooking for a family. When Bates and I were married, we entertained all the time. He preferred to have people over instead of going to a noisy restaurant. Then when Nicole was a teen-ager, I was 'Mama' to all her friends."

After dinner, the four of them sat around, enjoying each other's company. Bob and Mindy regaled them with tales of their adventures, glossing over the dangerous parts. Maybe Bob would share that with his father later. Maybe he wouldn't. He needed to talk with him about his latest cardiology report.

By the time they finished dinner, it was full on dark, as Hugh used to say. They took their whiskey out on the porch to watch the moonrise and pick out constellations. Before long, Bill and Nancy started yawning.

"We'll leave this to you all," he said, as the retrievers snored at their feet. "Bring the dogs in when you come." Elke was trying hard to relax, but there were so many new smells.

"Yes, sir, Dad. Nancy, thank you for a delicious dinner."

"Bob, you are more than welcome. Hope you all sleep well. I put an extra blanket out if you need it."

Bill kept the house too cold for her, but she didn't complain. She simply threw an extra blanket on her side of the bed. After the humidity of South America, the air conditioning felt divine to Bob and Mindy.

Nancy and Bill went arm-in-arm into The Lodge. Although Nancy had her own home close by, she stayed at The Lodge often. Bob didn't mind. He was happy for them. Her husband had died about the time Bob had gone to prison. They had lifted each other's spirits.

For the next week, Mindy and Bob laid low at The Retreat. With the emergency landing, coming home had been more of an ordeal than they had imagined. They slept in or napped in the afternoons. Mindy curled up in Bill's study to re-read some classics, while Bob looked over his notes from the production facility and tried to figure out the next steps.

Bill was surprised when Bob started bringing in the money packed in the plane. "How the heck did you manage that?" he asked.

Bob just smiled. Bill locked it all in the big old safe in The Lodge.

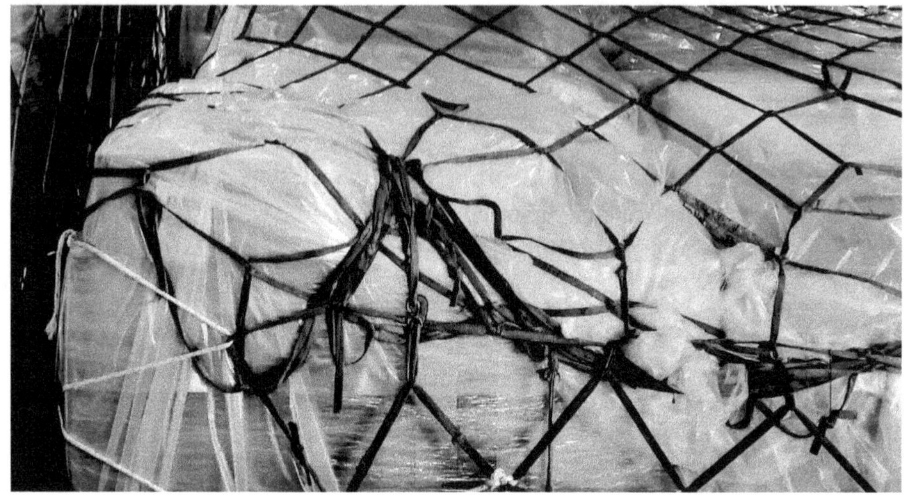

Nancy fixed them fantastic food and Bob and Mindy walked the dogs for Bill every day. Not only did he have Lincoln and Jefferson, but he had added two mutts to the pack. Bob was surprised. Bill always bought purebred dogs from the same breeder he'd worked with for years. But Nancy was an animal lover, and she'd rescued the new dogs from the pound. All the dogs got along. Brutus was a Jack Russell-Chihuahua mix who thought he was in charge, despite weighing 15 pounds to the retrievers' 100 pounds apiece. Dudley was one of those Heinz 57 dogs, just a slobbery mess. He had a skin condition that caused him to scratch and sneeze almost constantly, no matter what concoctions Nancy tried. Bless his canine heart. Bill loved each and every dog that showed up. He knew Nancy had a heart of gold, and The Retreat offered plenty of room for the dogs to roam.

Bob and Mindy's German Shepherd was very cautious at first and stuck close to Mindy, awaiting commands. She gave her the command to stand down and started throwing balls out into the grass. All the dogs loved that – a ball was irresistible, so they made tentative friendships, although Brutus was quite annoyed that he was not the center of attention.

Paul finally gets caught

Paul, Bob's felonious ex-brother-in-law, set up a financial consulting business with the money he'd stolen and started stealing from his new clients almost immediately. He reasoned that if he got away with it once, he could do it again.

What he didn't count on was one of his current clients talking to one of Bob's former partners, Dr. Young.

The two were out on the golf course one day when the talk turned to investments. That wasn't unusual because the men were in the same investment club. Paul handled the investments for Dr. Prem Patel, a local dentist.

Young said, "Hey, how about that stock we talked about at the last meeting? I really cleaned up. I made about $100,000."

"Wait a minute, what?" Patel said. "How much did you invest?"

"The same as always, $10,000."

"That's what I invested, but Paul said I only made $25,000."

Something in the back of Young's brain suddenly went into overdrive.

"Oh God. Your broker Paul was our business manager the whole time we thought we were making money hand over fist and ended up losing money because of Bob. Or so we thought. I knew that Bob couldn't have stolen that money. Oh man, this could be very bad."

Patel agreed.

“Listen, let’s keep this between ourselves for right now, okay? Just don’t invest anything else for the time being. Tell Paul your wife wants to install a pool or renovate the kitchen — anything to hold him off. I have someone I need to get in touch with about this,” Young said.

“Sure thing,” Patel said, and they finished their round, even though they were troubled by this revelation. Their scores reflected it.

When he got home later that afternoon, Young contacted Sam Williams, a high-school friend who had spent his career in the SBI. Williams referred him to a forensic accountant.

Within a week, the accountant called. Sure enough, Paul had done the exact same thing to the investment club that he’d done to the urology clinic.

The jig was up. Paul was finally going to be stopped and going to jail for a long time.

Young felt justified in taking Bob’s word for truth.

Once the rest of the urology team learned Bob was back in town, they invited him to the office for lunch one day. Bob was hesitant at first, nursing resentment for their total lack of support throughout his trial. Only Young had been helpful, along with Dr. Barber, both of whom had tested his new medication and apologized. The others had been largely silent. Now they said they wanted his forgiveness. Did they mean it?

He agreed to a meeting, because he wanted to get the feel of the group before he set anything in motion. Bob looked each in the eye before he answered. He’d learned a lot about lying from his time in prison.

"I needed all of you to believe me and defend me on that phony charge. I don't know why you – some of you – are still reluctant. I served five years in prison for something I didn't do. I was a good physician, I added a lot to this practice, and you just turned your heads.

"Thanks to Dr. Young and Dr. Barber, for learning to believe me and trust me. I need to know if that sentiment includes the rest of you."

The other partners looked uncomfortable. Bob had put them on the spot.

"Yes," both of them said. "We were wrong."

"And you're not just saying this because you want in on my new project?"

"If I get a hint of that," Young said, "actions will be taken."

The tension was rising.

"People make mistakes," Dr. Fisher said. "Dr. Allen and I judged too quickly. Bob, please, let's put this all behind us."

Then he accepted their apology, and they talked over sub sandwiches and Cheerwine.

"I knew I was being framed, but Paul was too slick for me. I couldn't prove it. Apology accepted."

"What can we do for you now, Bob?" Young asked, and the others nodded. "We'll do anything we can."

"You know, I want to keep working on this formula. I did well in South America. I think I may have something that we can expand to a wider customer base here in the States, maybe beyond."

The partners helped him set up a lab nearby, and even helped him invest, since his silent partner in South America was now out.

Bob patented his drug in the United States. It only needed a brief review from the FDA since it had been so successful in South America. Bob discovered he had a knack for developing urological-related pharmaceuticals. Maybe this would allow the practice members to make more money. He hoped so. He felt partially responsible for their losses, since he had hired Paul.

Bob and the partners started a corporation to manufacture the pharmaceuticals — the Endless Spring pills and gels being their flagship medications. Bob owned 60 percent of the company, and the four partners together owned 20. Mindy owned 10 percent, and Bob asked Bill to buy the remaining 10 percent.

They used Bill's 10 percent for start-up costs. Bob and Mindy had to start from scratch to build a new facility once they returned to the U.S.

They were up to the challenge.

Endless Spring

Bob and Mindy worked hard to re-establish the company stateside. Bob worked in research and development, while Mindy took over the marketing and public relations aspects. As always, they worked well together. Their medical knowledge dovetailed, while Mindy enjoyed her role as the "face" of the company. She didn't think of herself as beautiful, but she was always well put together— and she was the age of the Endless Spring demographic. Bob teased her that she was his spokesmodel.

After doing a lot of research and looking at myriad sites, they decided it made the most sense to open a manufacturing facility in Research Triangle Park, where innovation was the driver of many businesses. As Bob suspected, Endless Spring products took off in the U.S.

He not only had testimonials from his own experience, but also from his partners, as well as a few celebrities the Henderson family knew from North Carolina and beyond.

His old buddy Warden Solomon Dixon even gave him a testimonial. Thanks to Endless Spring, he and Marie had enjoyed many happy years together — really happy. He wasn't ashamed to say it, either. It mortified Marie because her bridge friends found out about it. It wasn't long, however, before their husbands — and some of the wives, truth be told — called Warden Dixon and asked how they could get their own prescriptions.

After a decade, Bob decided he was ready to get out of research and development. He and Mindy were about to turn 60, and both of them wanted to travel, to be free to go where they wanted to, when they wanted to, no restrictions. Prison time was so regimented, so limiting, and it takes years to stop feeling like the bars could close any minute. Their time in Argentina involved intense, focused work, with frequent thoughts about potential political unrest. They were always on their guard.

Bob developed an internship program that used recent graduates of Duke Medical School. At Mindy's urging and encouragement, he grudgingly hired graduates of UNC, Wake Forest, and East Carolina medical schools. The program grew to be an enormous success, with a full waiting list of applicants from each school.

Bob hired a program director, and he and Mindy began lecturing in Europe. Urologists there wanted to learn all about Endless Spring. Bob and Mindy lectured and traveled, setting their own schedule. They visited every European country before it was over with, and even made plans to visit China and Japan.

They thrived on the freedom of travel and the success of their product. No more cell walls, no more threats from anyone. Bob regained his reputation and built on it, but Mindy always reminded him to show humility. They had been blessed, by their upbringing, supportive family and friends, sheer good luck. Life was good and they were happy to share their fortunes with their employees and their families.

Bob and Mindy were relaxing in Paris, planning to take August off, since that was a popular vacation time on the continent.

Both of them were deeply shaken when Nancy called them. They'd had a lovely evening at The Ritz in Paris when the call came. Nancy kept it simple and direct: "Your father has died, Bob. It's time to come home, as quickly as you can."

The date was Aug. 2, 2005.

Bill had not told Bob that he had an aggressive form of

prostate cancer. Bob's partners were treating him and had agreed not to tell Bob until Bill was ready. But it was a virulent form, which spread quickly, despite the treatments.

Bill wanted Bob and Mindy to have their time together, enjoy success, live the life they wanted to. When the treatments became more intensive, he said to the doctors, "That's enough. I'm sure Bob would agree with me. Just let me pass quietly."

Bill never told Bob.

"Your father didn't want you to worry," Nancy said. "He wanted you to feel free to enjoy life after all you'd been through."

Bill had been out walking his dogs that afternoon and never came in for supper. Kent and his oldest son looked for him, and found him unconscious not far from the house, his faithful dogs lying quietly by his side.

Kent and his son rushed Bill to the hospital, where a couple of his poker buddies were waiting in the emergency room. Bill got the best care, but he never regained consciousness. His heart had simply stopped beating. His body was worn out.

After the initial shock, Bob told Nancy they'd get home as soon as they could. It took a day to get a flight from Paris to New York. After arriving in New York, they flew to Charlotte, where Kent's two oldest sons picked them up. Even though it was a bittersweet homecoming, Bob was glad to get back home to The Retreat.

Bill's funeral felt like Old Home Week — surviving classmates from Woodberry Forest and their families; Nancy's family; a contingent of the Ledford boys and their extended family, all "sported up" in coat and tie; Bob's friends from Woodberry and Duke; Bob's partners and their families; and all of the local business owners.

Bob, Mindy, and Nancy hosted a reception at the Country Club of Magnoliaville. Bill would have been proud. It was an afternoon full of reminiscing and reconnecting with people who had loved him. Hazel and her family came from Durham. Bob felt like she understood exactly how he was feeling.

Bill's estate was easy to settle because everything was already in Bob's name. When Bob, Mindy, and Nancy met with Bradford Winfield "Trey" Jacobs III, his father's attorney, Bob told him he wanted to create a significant memorial for Hugh and Bill. Trey suggested a park. There wasn't enough green space in McNeill County, he said. The three of them thought that was a great idea. It didn't take long for Henderson Park to be built. That amount of money from a single source makes things happen quickly.

The park would feature shaded gravel trails, benches and existing trees. Permanent plants would be added to grow over the years; annual flowers would lend a pop of color in every season. The plan outlined a fountain as the focal point at the center of the park. It would be modeled after the Pineapple Fountain in Charleston.

There was enough land for a senior center on one end of the park, and the committee suggested a concourse at the other end honoring veterans of all wars, since Bill had served in World War II.

After preliminary meetings with architects, the city, and the project manager, Bob and Mindy decided they'd stay home for a while to see work start on the park. Then they could go back to traveling, solely for pleasure, as long as they could.

Bob trusted Kent to be his eyes and ears on developments at the park until it was time for the finishing touches and the park's dedication.

Bob and Mindy each made a list of places they wanted to see and agreed to hit every spot they could. "We'll start with the ones we both want to visit," he said to Mindy. "Then we can alternate trips."

With careful planning, they managed to see almost everywhere they wanted to go, especially China, where Bob found ancient Chinese medicine absolutely fascinating. Mindy gravitated to the beautiful textiles of the region and bought silk scarves for Nancy and Hazel and Hazel's girls. The mountains in China gave Mindy a kind of peace she hadn't been expecting.

She and Bob felt satisfied and grateful after seeing so much of the world. They'd had a blast along the way, too, and it soothed the worst part of Bob's grief. They spent a lot of their money, but the estate was already worth a hefty sum, and Bob could hear his grandfather say, "Hell, you can't take it with you."

When they finally came home to The Retreat, it felt so right to Bob. Even though the memory of that horrible night Buck died never left him, Bob felt like he'd paid his dues during those five years in prison.

The Retreat was home, a safe place, a place where he could find forgiveness and love. Hugh and Bill had always wanted to do the best, right thing.

Bob wanted to focus on that. It was time to let go of the sadness from the past. Since he'd barely known his mother, he didn't miss her. He had loved his sister, Liz, as best he could – barely knowing her, either.

Now was Bob's time to enjoy his life with Mindy, knowing they had created something people wanted to make their lives more pleasurable.

Like his father and grandfather before him, Bob loved this land and what they had made from it.

Settling down

Mindy made few changes at The Retreat. She redecorated the master suite with some of the things they had accumulated and added pieces from their travels in the living room, dining room and sunroom.

There was no need for pots, pans, plates and the like but Bob decided to update some of the furniture that had been well used over the years.

Bill's dogs had gone to live with Kent while the couple traveled, and both had since crossed the rainbow bridge. Nancy went with Bob and Mindy to the shelter where they adopted a small spaniel mix to keep them company.

Mindy talked to Hazel about setting up a nursing scholarship at Watts College of Nursing in Durham. They agreed it would be named the Henderson Nursing Scholarship.

Bob followed the procedure as Nancy worked on it and designated part of his estate for a scholarship at Woodberry Forest and one at Duke University.

Kent encouraged Bob to write a short history of The Retreat to be used when the property went into trust, as Bill and Bob had planned. "You're the last of the Hendersons, and someone needs to gather that information," Kent said.

With Nancy's connections at the library, Bob got to work. Using newspaper clippings and talking to people who had known Bill, even folks who remembered Hugh, he started to form an outline of the family history. The more he discovered, the more connections he made, the happier he got. He truly appreciated how his family had changed their county, how Hugh had grown the family's presence through hard work and natural abilities.

Again, he faced the specter of Buck, but that was a story that would never be told. Lucy Athena had long since retired; her son was now the coroner. She was nearing 100 but remained as bright as ever. The community turned to her for advice and knowledge of the past. She learned about Bob's project and asked him to visit her.

A sharp pain ran through Bob's chest, but he appeared when summoned. She said nothing about Buck, but they exchanged looks that said the knowledge was still fresh.

"I want to tell you some of the things your grandfather did for Magnoliaville, things that few white men would have done in those days. He was as fine a man as I ever met."

Her stories filled out rich details about things Hugh had done, things few people knew about. Bob found himself at Lucy Athena's house often, drinking strong coffee and devouring her stories.

Mindy was Bob's first reader, and she helped him organize his information. People at the library put him in touch with an editor and designer who could help him build a short book of family history.

It was one of the most satisfying things he'd done. Maybe there would be no more Hendersons, but they wouldn't be forgotten, at least for a little while.

Photo by Sean Meyers Photography

80th birthday - 2020

Mindy and Bob were sitting on the porch one day, enjoying the warm air and relaxing.

"I've not said it enough," she said, "but you have given me a life beyond anything I ever imagined. I thought after the disaster of my first marriage and the time in prison, life would be just one struggle after another.
"When you approached me at that meeting so long ago, I never imagined I could find happiness and real fulfillment in my future."

Bob took her hand. "I couldn't have done any of this without you. I'd lost so many people; I'd had so many failed relationships with women, from my mother to my ex-wife. I figured I was meant to go it alone, until I saw that you were willing to trust me, at least a little."

“We’ve made good lives,” Mindy said.

“I think we’ve made a difference. I think we’re going to leave a legacy we can be proud of,” Bob said. “I love you.”

A few weeks later, on the morning of Bob’s 80th birthday, Oct. 1, he met with his attorney — Bradford Winfield “Jake” Jacobs IV — his grandfather’s attorney’s grandson — to sign papers with attorneys from the Conservation Trust of North Carolina. At Bob’s death, The Retreat would become a conference center with an emphasis on environmental and conservation issues. The remainder of the property would be protected in perpetuity. Kent, Katie, and their four sons and their sons’ families would remain on the land as long as they chose, the job of caretaker being passed down to the sons and grandsons. Jake had worked hard to draw up the plans and file the paperwork, and this was the final step. Bob felt good that he was protecting his land. As his grandfather Hugh always said, they weren’t making any more.

Bob’s birthday party was an unforgettable evening. Mindy threw a dinner for him with their close friends and his former partners. Everything was perfect. They had a shrimp boil — one of Bob’s favorite meals. Everything was starting to open up after the pandemic, and they had a lovely dinner out in the front yard under a spacious white tent. The weather couldn’t have been better for October.

The guests had gone home. Mindy went up to bed. Bob sipped a last glass of whiskey, sitting on the porch in a rocker that his grandfather once sat in. Cooler air settled around him — a good time to reflect on life, he thought. Like anyone else, he’d been through good and bad, and he’d decided long ago that he wouldn’t change a thing. It had been a great adventure.

The evening deepened. He closed his eyes and heard

Joe barking in the distance, the sweet sound of Hazel's melodious laughter. That's when he knew his daddy and granddaddy would be along soon for him. That seemed just fine. He was at peace.

HAP ROBERTS

Following a successful career at Food Town Stores, Inc., later Food Lion, Hap Roberts opened his own CPA firm in 1983. A year later, he and his wife, Annette, founded Statewide Title, Inc. and through the years he served on numerous philanthropic boards as well as nineteen years on the corporate board of Ryans Family Steakhouses, Inc.

In 2018, he was ready for a completely different challenge, and thus embarked on writing his memoirs.

Hap followed "Everybody Was Happy" with "Mimosa," a memoir by his uncle, Ralph Roberts, that he shepherded to publication after finding more than a dozen different copies of Ralph's manuscript.

"The Cotton Broker's Son" is Hap's first novel.

Hap and Annette live in Salisbury with their beloved dogs, Elke the German Shepherd and Lilli the Yorkie. Their daughter, Heather Brady, lives just a few doors down from her parents with her husband, Brad, and their children, Bell and Graham.

www.ingramcontent.com/pod-product-compliance
Lightning Source LLC
Chambersburg PA
CBHW070553310726
48982CB00011B/1570/J